Field of
PLEASURE

FARRAH ROCHON

KIMANI
ROMANCE

Dedicated to the amazing staff of St. Elizabeth's Hospital.
Thank you for all that you have done for my family.

"…for I am the Lord, who heals you…"
—*Exodus* 15:26

KIMANI PRESS™

ISBN-13: 978-0-373-86227-6

FIELD OF PLEASURE

Copyright © 2011 by Farrah Roybiskie

Recycling programs
for this product may
not exist in your area.

www.kimanipress.com

Printed in U.S.A.

"Shhh," he whispered into the hair just above her ear.

He resumed his gentle caress up and down her back, his fingers tingling from the warmth. "I told you everything would be okay, didn't I?"

"Yes, you did," Chyna murmured against his chest. She lifted her head and stared into his eyes. "Thank you."

The words were so soft, Jared barely heard them. Or maybe her voice just seemed hushed because he could hardly hear anything past the blood pounding in his ears.

Gazing at him with those brilliant gray eyes that would put Bambi to shame, Chyna slipped her hand up his neck, her fingertips applying gentle pressure at the base of his head. She tilted her face up, and it was all the invitation he needed. Jared lowered his mouth and connected with hers.

The supple give of her soft lips sent a jolt of desire shooting through his body. He glided his hand up her spine to the back of her head, holding her in place while he melded his lips to hers. He couldn't take a second more of this closed-mouth business. Prying her lips open with his tongue, Jared plunged inside.

Good God, she tasted like heaven.

He swallowed Chyna's low moan and pulled her tighter, needing to feel her against him. It was no use denying the arousal hardening just beyond his zipper. If she didn't see how much he wanted her, she damn sure could feel it.

Books by Farrah Rochon

Kimani Romance

Huddle with Me Tonight
I'll Catch You
Field of Pleasure

FARRAH ROCHON

had dreams of becoming a fashion designer as a teenager, until she discovered she would be expected to wear something other than jeans to work every day. Thankfully, the coffee shop where she writes does not have a dress code.

When Farrah is not penning stories, the avid sports fan feeds her addiction to football by attending New Orleans Saints games.

Dear Reader,

First, I must admit that I am both humbled and thrilled at the overwhelming response to my New York Sabers series. It warms my heart to know that readers have come to love my sexy football players as much as I do.

The third installment, *Field of Pleasure,* features laid-back, fun-loving cornerback Jared Dawson. Many readers have asked me if Jared would get his own book since he seems to already have everything going for him. Jared has the perfect job, the perfect girlfriend, the perfect life…until it all comes crashing down around him.

It takes a strong woman to help lift Jared out of the dark place he finds himself in, and I believe Chyna McCray is one of the strongest heroines I've ever written. She is Jared's perfect match in every way. I have a feeling this couple will win over many hearts.

Contact me on Facebook, Twitter or at my website, www.farrahrochon.com, to let me know what you think of *Field of Pleasure.* And stay tuned for the next book in the series! Finally, Theo Stokes and Deirdre Smallwood get their own story.

All the best,

Farrah Rochon

Chapter 1

Ensconced in a plush velvet chair, Jared Dawson observed the LCD screen with disdain as the punt returner for the New England Patriots was brought down at the eighteenth yard line.

"Pitiful," he huffed. "At least get it to the twenty." He brought a cut crystal tumbler glass to his lips, mumbling, "I would have taken it to the house," before downing a generous portion of the casino's top-shelf Scotch.

Every seat in the ultra exclusive Players Club at Atlantic City's Rio Grande Casino was taken. It was the biggest gambling day of the year—Super Bowl Sunday—and everyone wanted a piece of the action. Jared glanced over at the craps table, able to gauge who was winning and who would have to take out a new mortgage on their house just by studying the players' body language. He'd been on both sides of that coin before.

He could *not* go back there.

Which was why, for about the thousandth time this hour, Jared asked himself just what in the hell he was doing in this casino.

He usually wasn't one for self-sabotage, but that was the only reasonable explanation he could find in a mind that was marinating in more alcohol than he usually consumed in a month.

One of the conditions of his agreement with the New York Sabers, the NFL team that should have been playing in today's Super Bowl, was that he steer clear of all gaming establishments. Even though Jared had never gambled on a Sabers game, the bet he'd placed on a Raiders-Broncos matchup a few years ago was enough to get him thrown out of the league for life. The NFL had a strict policy on employees gambling on NFL games. It wasn't tolerated. Ever.

Sabers upper management had decided to keep the incident in-house and not report him to the league, but Jared had been required to meet with the team's shrink for months to ensure that his betting wasn't due to a more serious gambling addiction. He had signed an agreement promising to refrain from all forms of gambling. For the past three years, he'd done his best to honor that agreement. Other than the occasional game of zero-stakes poker when his teammates grew tired of their weekly dominoes game, he hadn't come remotely close to anything to do with gambling.

But every man had his breaking point.

Losing in the first round of the playoffs had been a crushing blow, but this wasn't the first time the Sabers had come up short. They always had next year, and at thirty years old, Jared figured he still had another five years in the league, easy. It was walking into his hotel room six months ago to find his girlfriend of ten years—the love of his life—Samantha Miller, in bed with his recently traded ex-teammate Carlos Garcia that had nearly sent Jared over the edge.

Jared slipped his right hand into his pocket and fingered the five-carat radiant cut diamond he'd envisioned sliding on Samantha's finger today. The fantasy had played out a dozen times in his dreams. Amid the confetti and thousands of roaring fans, he would drop to one knee and pop the question. And because it was *his* fantasy, he, of course, would have just scored the game-winning touchdown to give the Sabers their first Super Bowl win.

But it hadn't happened that way, had it?

Instead, he was watching the big game on television like everyone else, while Carlos was doing only God knew what with the woman Jared had given ten years of his life to.

For a split second he had contemplated an assault, but he didn't want his mom to have to explain to her friends that her son was being tried for a criminal case. Instead, Jared had set out to do a little self-destruction. He was one Scotch away from killing his liver and one bet away from flushing his career down the toilet.

As the normally fifteen-minute halftime show stretched into a thirty-minute glitz-filled concert, Jared pushed himself up from his seat and, with glass in hand, strolled around the casino's private club. In the far right corner a high-stakes poker game was in progress. A familiar tingle inched along his skin as the tension radiating from the table seeped into his bones. He closed his eyes, taking deep breaths, recalling the rush of excitement laying down that first bet always induced.

He needed to step away. Now.

Before he reached his hand into his pocket and drew out his wallet.

Before he slid his black American Express to the pit boss and made an irrevocable mistake that would cost him so much more than whatever money he would lose at the craps table.

Jared didn't get a chance to make another move. A set of strong fingers gripped his biceps and spun him around so fast that Scotch sloshed over the rim of his glass.

"What the hell?" Jared barked.

"That's my question," Torrian Smallwood, ex-wide receiver and current assistant coach with the Sabers, growled. He was also one of Jared's best friends. It didn't surprise him that Torrian had tracked him down.

"Are you out of your mind?" Torrian bit out. "You *trying* to ruin your life?"

"Maybe." Jared washed the flippant answer down with the remainder of his Scotch.

Torrian's gaze darted around their immediate area. Grabbing Jared's arm, he tugged him to a darkened corner where they were partially shielded by burgundy curtains.

"Why don't you think about someone other than yourself for a minute?" Torrian snapped.

"Aren't you and the rest of the guys always telling me I need to stop taking care of everybody else and start taking care of myself for a change?" he snarled.

"Don't give me that, Jared. This is irresponsible and you know it. You have an entire team counting on you. Hell, I'm missing the Super Bowl running after you."

"I didn't ask you to come here," Jared stated.

"I've been waiting for something like this to happen. You've been living on the brink of destruction for months now." Torrian ran an agitated hand down his face, frustration evident in his tightly clenched jaws. "Look, I know what went down with Samantha hurt you, but don't do this to yourself. You've worked too hard at getting things right with the team. Don't throw it away."

It was the concern in his teammate's eyes that did Jared in. Torrian cared enough to track him all the way to Atlantic City in an attempt to save his sorry ass, when Jared wasn't so sure it was even worth saving. It was the kind of devotion only men who'd been through the fire together could share.

"How could she do that to me?" Jared choked out. "After everything—"

Unable to hold his emotions in check a second longer, Jared tumbled into his friend's arms and sobbed out the agonizing heartache of a betrayal handed to him by a woman he'd loved more than life itself.

Fingers planted on the running track's rubber surface, Jared focused his eyes on the white flag that marked forty yards. He counted down with the trainer as he got on his mark, set and took off down the track. In less time than it would take to write his full name, he was putting on the brakes. Jared checked the stopwatch. He'd improved his time by three tenths of a second, but he still needed to cut another five.

After where he'd been just six weeks ago, when Torrian found him wallowing in Scotch and on the verge of ruining his career, Jared was grateful to even be back here at the Sabers' practice facility. But having this second chance wasn't enough for him. He had to *do* something with it. He would show the team he was one hundred percent in this, which was why he was determined to run the forty in under four-point-four seconds by the start of next season. He still had the rest of the off-season and training camp to make that happen.

"You…do all right…for an old guy," his fellow teammate Randall Robinson said through several pauses while he tried to catch his breath.

"Better than you," Jared countered with a playful jab to Randall's shoulder.

"That's why I'm here instead of lounging on a beach somewhere. I can't afford to spend the off-season fooling around."

"I hear you," Jared said. "I need the extra conditioning."

And the reservation he'd made for a monthlong engagement celebration in Cabo San Lucas was in both his and Samantha's name. Right now it was more tempting to drink battery acid than make a solo trip to Mexico.

Jared figured that enough players used the excuse of wanting to buff up during the off-season that no one would give his opting to do so a second thought. But he worked with some savvy men, and those who had known him for a while saw right through his crap.

Randall was one of them.

His teammate clamped a hand on Jared's shoulder and gave him a commiserating squeeze. "I've been meaning to ask how you're doing, man. That was cold what Carlos did to you. I don't know how you stopped yourself from kicking his ass."

Easy. Jared had been too enraged to do anything but storm out of the room. He'd had two choices that night: leave or pummel his ex-teammate.

Six months later, and he still remembered every disgusting detail. Samantha's shocked gasp when he'd walked into his hotel room two hours earlier than he'd been expected to return and found her naked and straddling his former teammate. The floor littered with their clothes, pillows and linens. Carlos's smug smile as he'd stared at Jared from the bed. The scene would be forever etched into his mind.

"I'm over it," Jared lied.

"After all the time you and Sam were together?" The look Randall shot him was the very definition of incredulous. Yeah, some of his teammates knew him all too well.

"Fine, I'm still pissed," Jared admitted as he marched down the sideline of the enclosed practice field. "But I'd be more upset with myself if I had acted a fool over her. Sam made her choice. I'm dealing with it."

"You need any help dealing with it?" Randall asked as they came upon a table with a half dozen Gatorade dispensers and stacks of folded towels.

Jared snatched a towel and ran it over his face and neck, mopping the sweat from his skin. "What kind of help?"

Randall nodded toward the far right side of the practice field, where a pretty awesome display of female flesh danced to one of the songs that usually played during timeouts at Sabers home games. The team's cheerleading/dance squad, the Saberrettes, was working hard.

He had to admit, even without the barely there outfits they donned for the games, every single one of the girls was smokin' hot. Jared had always taken a barely-look-and-never-*ever*-touch approach when it came to the Saberrettes. He'd been one hundred percent faithful to Samantha from the minute they'd officially started dating back in their sophomore year at San Diego State.

"I don't know about that," Jared said. "You know the team has a no-fraternizing rule when it comes to cheerleaders."

"Man, nobody pays attention to that rule. What's the big deal?" Randall shrugged. "I'm not suggesting you propose marriage. Just, you know, try hooking up for a night or two."

Jared's first instinct was to tell his teammate he wasn't interested in "hooking up." Hell, he'd been with the same woman for so long, he didn't even know *how* to have casual sex. But as the image of Carlos clutching Samantha's naked back flashed in his head—something that still occurred way too often—Jared reconsidered Randall's suggestion. At least a night out with a beautiful woman would give him something else to think about.

"I need to call the day care and check in on my little man," Randall said. "Give me fifteen minutes, and then we can try the forty again."

As he watched his teammate jog across the field, Jared felt the familiar twinge of envy that pulled at his chest whenever he thought about Randall and his two-year-old son, Christopher. The guy was brave as hell, fighting his lunatic ex-girlfriend for custody and raising his son on his own. Jared didn't envy Randall going at it alone, but he would have given just about anything to have a son.

Samantha had never wanted kids. She'd never made much of a push to get married, either. Made perfect sense to him now. It was so much easier to break off a ten-year relationship than to dissolve a marriage.

Jared bit back a curse and turned his attention to the smorgasbord of firm thighs, surgically enhanced breasts and mile-long legs on full display across the field. As much as it would do his body some good, he wasn't all that interested in hooking up for a couple of nights of casual sex, especially with a member of the team's dance squad. What would happen once they'd had their fun?

At least with someone he met in a club the chances of

ever seeing the woman again would be slight. He wasn't sure he could handle running into someone he'd slept with and just pretending nothing had happened between them.

Then again, if one of the Saberrettes was game for a little naked Twister, what was the harm? After what he'd been through these past six months, he was due for a bit of pleasurable entertainment.

Jared filled his paper cup with Gatorade and tipped his head back, downing the drink in one long gulp. He looked up and nearly choked on the liquid he'd just swallowed. Heading toward him was easily one of the hottest, most drop-dead gorgeous women he'd ever laid eyes on.

She strode confidently across the practice field's artificial turf, carrying an empty plastic water bottle in each hand.

She was absolutely stunning, her creamy skin like milk with a hint of coffee swirled in. She had a dancer's body, tight and toned. But it was her exotic gray eyes that nearly dropped him to his knees. They were mesmerizing and mysterious, and had Jared taking a second to catch his breath.

As she approached, a pleasant but innocuous smile drew across her face. "Hi," she said with a polite nod. "Just coming over to steal Gatorade."

"By all means," Jared said, going for smooth. "Feel free to help yourself to anything you see here." Okay, that was lame as hell.

She thought so, too. The smile pulling at the corner of her mouth said she was more amused than charmed by his blatant come-on.

Man, he was out of practice. He didn't know any new pickup lines, and something told him the ones he'd used back in college wouldn't go over so well.

"Excuse me," Gray Eyes said as she reached for the second jug.

Jared stepped out of her way. "Looks like you girls are practicing pretty hard over there," he tried.

"This isn't a practice. It's an audition for potential new members for the squad."

"Oh, tryouts. Cool." When she didn't offer anything further, Jared continued. "I'm sorry I don't know your name. I'm not familiar with all the girls on the squad."

She swung that gorgeous mane of hair over her shoulder as she straightened from her crouch at the table, twisting the cap on the second bottle of pilfered Gatorade. "Actually, I'm not on the squad," she answered. She stretched a hand out. "I'm Chyna, with a *Y* not an *I*. I was brought in to choreograph some new routines for the Saberrettes."

"Nice to meet you, Chyna with a *Y*," he said, capturing the hand she'd offered. Her skin was baby-smooth. Even after she'd released his grip, a warm tingle remained imprinted on his palm.

"So, you're a professional choreographer?" Jared asked.

"Professional enough," she said. "I'm a good friend of Liani Dixon, who *is* a member of the Saberrettes. She recommended me." She glanced over at the group of dancers. "I really should get back." Grasping the handles of both jugs, she turned to leave.

"Hold up," Jared said, reaching for her arm.

She stopped, peered at his hand, then leveled him with a stare that clearly said he'd crossed a line. Jared dropped his hand, but not his campaign to keep up their conversation.

"At least let me help you carry these," he said, reaching for the jugs.

"I can manage," she replied and turned once again in the direction of the dance squad.

"Is there a reason you're blowing me off?" Jared called after her.

"Well, I *am* working, and to be honest, I'm just not interested," she said. "Try not to take it personally," she called over her shoulder, not bothering to turn around.

As he watched her perfectly shaped rear end saunter away, Jared couldn't help but take it personally. He'd thought the hardest part about deciding to take the plunge would be in summoning the motivation to actually ask a woman out. He had never considered getting shot down. And there was no mistaking what had just happened here: he'd been shot down, but good.

It confused him. And intrigued him.

A smile hitched up the corner of his mouth as he watched her strut across the field.

Wait. He was smiling?

It had been so long since he'd had anything to smile about, Jared was surprised his facial muscles even remembered the mechanics. But there was no mistaking the tug he felt pulling at the corners of his mouth. Maybe there was something to this diversion thing after all.

Chapter 2

Chyna McCrea tried to concentrate on the nineteen-year-old blonde who had incorporated every trick she'd learned from high school cheerleading camp into the routine she was performing. But after enduring the endless parade of girls who'd *kicked-stepped-kicked* their way across the field today, Chyna had a hard time staying focused.

And if she could convince herself to believe that, she had a nice island in the Bahamas for sale.

Her focus had been just fine up until the moment she went on a Gatorade run and encountered Jared Dawson. The man was drool-worthy; there was no denying that. There was not an ounce of flab anywhere. Like many of his teammates, his physique had been honed by countless practices and conditioning, much like what he was doing today. He wasn't bulked up with steroid-enhanced muscles. His were leaner; well-defined, but not overstated.

Oh, yeah, drool-worthy definitely fit the bill.

And he'd just tried hitting on her.

Oh. My. *God.*

Her heart started that boom, boom, pow thing again, and Chyna had to grip the edge of the folding table where she and the Saberrettes' cocaptains sat.

Her best friend, Liani Dixon, who at three years on the squad was considered a senior member, had shared the scoop regarding the drama that had happened at an away game last season, when Jared had caught his ex-girlfriend with another Sabers player. Chyna had felt sorry for him then, but after meeting the man face-to-face she now felt sorry for his ex-girlfriend. The woman was obviously a few twirls short of a double pirouette to cheat on a guy like Jared Dawson.

"Helloooo. Earth to Chyna."

Startled out of her dream lust, Chyna turned to Kenya Simmons, one of the squad's cocaptains. "What do you think?" Kenya asked.

"Sorry about that," Chyna said. "I had something else on my mind." Six feet four inches of football-playing yumminess, to be exact.

"What did you think about the last group of girls?" Kenya asked again with a subtle bite to her tone.

Chyna's first impulse was to bite back, but she knew she was wrong here. She'd been hired to assist the Saberrettes, not daydream about one of the Sabers. Chyna sifted through the applications and attached score sheets, trying to find something positive to point out. It wasn't easy.

"The last girl was okay—at least she had *some* athletic ability—but no one really impressed me in the one-on-one interviews. These girls seem to want all of the glamour, but none of the work." She tossed the stack of papers onto the table. "I've watched Liani as she's cheered with the squad these past three years and I know that being a Saberrette is more than just a great body and a pretty smile. You all pride yourselves on being a squad with substance, and I can't see the majority of those girls giving up a Saturday morning to conduct a dance camp at the YMCA."

"Not unless they were paid to do it," Kenya said. She grinned. "I still love the shock on their faces when they hear this job only pays seventy-five dollars a game."

"And not a penny for practices," Liani griped from the other end of the table. It was her friend's biggest bone of contention with being a Saberrette. Though Liani wasn't necessarily hard up for cash. Not only was she the daughter of a wealthy lawyer, but she also took full advantage of the many paid appearances the dance squad was asked to do throughout the year.

"Maybe this next group will be better." Kenya nodded toward the six girls coming their way.

Chyna's attention quickly moved from the girls to the group of players just beyond them. And one player in particular—who was staring directly at her.

Oh, Lord. Her heart quivered with a flurry of excitement.

Was this some kind of joke; maybe something Liani had set up? She was the only person who knew that in their private game of If-You-Could-Score-with-a-Saber-Who-Would-You-Choose, Chyna always, always, *always* chose Jared Dawson.

She glanced at her best friend, searching for even a hint of a grin. But Liani was completely clueless, her focus on the six Saberrette hopefuls ready to give it their best shot.

With a shaky breath, Chyna's eyes once again wandered

to the left side of the field house. Jared was high-stepping through a row of evenly spaced rubber tires, his powerful body moving at lightning speed through the obstacle.

Maybe she had read too much into their earlier exchange. Maybe he was just being a nice guy. Just because he'd asked her name and offered to carry a couple of jugs of Gatorade didn't mean he was interested in her.

She chanced another quick glance over there and found him staring again, directly at her. His mouth widened in a huge smile.

Oh, *Lord.*

Jared pressed the rewind button on the remote control, scrolling back to the previous play in which he'd missed an easy interception in last season's playoff game. On the next play, the Detroit Lions scored a touchdown and took the lead.

He hit the button again, studying the screen. He knew what he'd done wrong. He had taken his eyes off the ball, his mind already jumping to the route he would run after the interception. Just one problem with that; he didn't make the catch.

"You do love self-torture, don't you?"

The lights in the film room snapped on and Torrian came strolling in. Jared blinked rapidly, trying to adjust to the bright halogen bulbs.

Torrian snatched the remote and scrolled back to the play Jared had watched at least two dozen times. Leaning a hip against the table, his ex-teammate pointed at the screen. "You know what you did wrong, don't you? You took your eyes off the ball…"

"Off the ball," Jared said along with him.

"Maybe you should start practicing with the wide receivers. I teach my guys how to keep their concentration on the ball."

"I play defense and special teams. I'm not going over to the dark side," Jared said.

The jawing between the Sabers cornerbacks and wide receivers was legendary. Wide receivers claimed the cornerback position was for guys who didn't have the hands to succeed at wide receiver. The cornerbacks' response was usually not suitable for delicate ears. It made for some spirited trash talk in the Sabers locker room.

"Your loss." Torrian tossed the remote on the table. "Hey, you up for dominoes tonight? Cedric and Payton are still floating around the Caribbean, but Theo will be in town. You game?"

"Why not?" Jared shrugged. "Not as if I've got anything better to do."

Torrian's brow creased with concern. "Maybe playing dominoes with the guys isn't the best thing for you this weekend. Why don't you go to a club or something? Try to meet somebody, man. It's been six months."

Jared winced at the reminder. "I don't do clubs, and I'm not up to meeting anybody," he said. "You guys are worse than a bunch of high school girls with this matchmaking crap."

"Who else is matchmaking?"

"Robinson," Jared groused.

"Who said my name?" Randall asked, strolling into the room. He slapped palms with Torrian and took the seat next to Jared. "Don't tell me you're studying that missed interception *again*. Dude, it was one play. Let it go."

"It led to our biggest loss of the year," Jared reminded him.

Randall expelled a disparaging sigh. "So, you got a date or what?"

"Doesn't look like it," Jared answered. "I got knocked down worse than you did." He pointed at the screen, where Randall had just taken a punishing blow from one of the Lions' defenders.

"You struck out with a Saberrette? That's a new low." Randall chuckled.

"Wait. You asked out one of the cheerleaders?" Torrian's eyes widened in amused surprise. His cell phone started chiming and he looked at the screen. "I need to take this call." He pointed at Jared as he backed out of the film room. "I want to hear about this tonight."

Jared's lips thinned with irritation. How had he become the butt of jokes about dating troubles?

Ah, right. Lying, cheating ex-girlfriend humping a fellow teammate in his hotel bed. No one was likely to forget *that* anytime soon.

"What went wrong?" Randall asked. "That should have been the easiest hookup ever."

"First, it's not as if I was prepared to duck into the equipment room and 'hook up' on the spot," Jared drawled. "And secondly, I didn't ask one of the cheerleaders. It was the choreographer they just hired."

"There's a new girl?" One of Randall's brows spiked with interest.

"Yes, and don't even think about it," Jared said.

"Why not? You already struck out. Maybe I'd have better luck. We both know I'm better at this stuff than you are."

Jared rolled his eyes.

"So, which one are you going after next?" Randall asked.

"Would you stop talking about these girls as if they're interchangeable?"

"I didn't say they were interchangeable," Randall argued. He twisted around in his seat to face Jared head-on. "I don't think you understand the point of this experiment. You shouldn't try to jump right back into a potential ten-year relationship. Have some fun, man. Burn off some energy." Randall held two fingers up as if he were conducting an orchestra. "Say it with me— this is a diversion," he finished in a sing-songy voice, dragging out the last word. "You should try again," his teammate encouraged.

Jared's mouth dipped in an annoyed frown. "I'll have to think about it." He picked up the remote and hit the fast-forward button. "If you'd seen the way she turned those gray eyes on me, you probably would change your tune."

"Gray eyes?" Randall slapped both hands flat on the table "Hold on. Is her name Chyna?"

Jared's head snapped back in surprise. "Yeah, you know her?"

"She's friends with one of the other girls on the squad. I've seen her at the sports bar where the team hangs out after home games. Of course, you wouldn't know because you and the rest of the Four Musketeers have your own thing after home games," Randall grunted.

Jared knew the other guys on the team were jealous of the bond between him, Torrian, Cedric and Theo.

Too bad, bro. Not everyone can belong.

"Tell me what you know about her," Jared prodded.

Randall shrugged. "She's hot and all, but she seems kind of boring. I think her nickname is Brainiac or The Brain, or something like that. Definitely not fling material."

"The Brain?" Jared's brow raised a fraction. "What's that about?"

"She's, you know, smart and stuff. And she's way too serious. I doubt she even knows the meaning of fun," Randall continued, picking up the remote and fast-forwarding through more tape. "Forget about Chyna. She's not going to give you any." He leaned in and shot a quick glance toward the door. In a conspiratory whisper, he said, "From what I hear, Haley and Tamika know how to have a good time. Ask one of them out. I promise you'll get laid before the end of the night."

Jared shot his teammate a wary look. "Do me a favor. When it's time to explain the birds and bees to little Christopher, call me. You're just going to corrupt your son's mind."

Two hours later, as he was making his way out of the Sabers practice compound, Jared faltered as he spotted "The Brain" waiting just inside the double glass doors. She'd pulled a pair of purple sweats over those super-short cutoffs she'd been wearing earlier. And wasn't that a damn shame.

She'd spotted him. Jared could tell by the way her shoulders stiffened and how she immediately found something fascinating to look at outside the door. She probably thought he would try to strike up a conversation again.

She was right.

Something about the way she blew him off without giving him a second glance intrigued the heck out of him. Maybe that was the appeal: her playing-hard-to-get attitude made it unlikely he'd get anywhere with her. He could convince himself that he'd tried to move on from Samantha; it wasn't his fault it hadn't worked.

But as he approached Chyna, Jared's mind, for once,

wasn't on his ex-girlfriend. Something Randall said had bothered him. He'd described her as not knowing the meaning of fun. She worked with cheerleaders, for goodness sake. Fun was in the job description, wasn't it?

Jared wasn't sure why, but the thought of her being so serious to the point that it was part of her reputation got to him. Someone that young, that downright gorgeous, should know how to kick back and enjoy herself.

"Hi again," Jared greeted.

She turned her attention from outside, offering him an indifferent smile that still managed to snatch the air from his lungs.

"Hi," she answered.

When she hefted the nylon duffel bag more securely over her shoulder and averted her attention again, Jared nearly gave up. But, damn, he didn't want to. He needed to know why she dismissed him out of hand. What was he doing wrong?

"Any luck with the tryouts?" he tried.

"A little," she answered, then said nothing else.

Okay, clearly he needed to brush up on his flirting skills, but he didn't have time for that now. Jared had a feeling she was ready to bolt at any second. He decided to cut to the chase.

"What is it about me that you don't like?" he asked, and even as he said it he realized how arrogant he sounded. As if she had to have a reason for not liking him. Maybe she just didn't. Reason unnecessary.

She surprised him when she said, "Nothing."

"Wait, so do you mean there is nothing that you *like* about me, or there's nothing you *don't* like about me?"

And now he had confused himself.

"There's nothing I don't like about you," she answered, that smile becoming a little more genuine. Why that made him feel so good, he didn't know, but he liked the fact that he'd put a smile on her face. "I told you earlier not to take it personally. The Saberrettes have a rule against consorting with the ball players. Since I'm working alongside them, I should abide by the same rules they do."

"Yeah, but that no-fraternizing rule is ignored more than the Sabers' rule on not taking anything from the field house." Jared held up the roll of Ace bandages he'd snatched from the equipment room to prove his point. "Believe me, there's definitely some fraternizing going on."

Her features softened, her eyes crinkling at the corners as an easy grin pulled at her lips. "Sorry, but I'm a bit of a rule follower."

God, that smile of hers was devastating. It stirred things inside him that hadn't stirred in months.

"Well, it's the off-season," Jared said, feeling a little more confident with each second that smile remained on her lips. Maybe his flirting skills weren't as rusty as he'd first thought. "There's nothing against some friendly conversation during the off-season, is there?"

She hesitated for the barest moment, before saying, "That's...not a good idea."

She looked beyond his shoulder and gave a two-finger wave to someone coming up the hallway. A second later, Liani Dixon, one of the few members of the dance squad Jared knew by name, bounded up to them.

"Sorry that took so long," she said to Chyna. Liani looked from him to Chyna, and then back to him. She held out her hand. "I'm Liani," she greeted. "I don't think we've ever officially met."

Jared shook her hand. "No, we haven't."

The only reason he knew her name was because she

was one of those Saberrettes who had ignored the no-fraternizing rule last season when she'd hooked up with Randall the night before one of the Sabers' away games. Funny thing is his teammate had given up her name only after Jared had pried the information out of him, and Randall had never brought the incident up again. The one time Liani's name had surfaced in locker-room talk, when one of the rookies mentioned that he'd like to hit that, Randall had nearly taken the guy's head off.

"I feel bad not knowing more of you by name," Jared admitted. "I don't attend many team functions outside of the regular game and practice, so I haven't had a chance to meet all of the Saberrettes. I appreciate what you all do for the team, though."

He looked at Chyna, hoping his compliment would earn him another one of those sexy smiles, but the swift dip in her brow was as far from a smile as you could get. Jared recalled the conversation on fraternizing they'd been engaged in right before Liani joined them, and he understood. "What you all do for the team" had a different connotation when he looked at it that way.

"I meant the cheering," he clarified, earning a confused look from Liani.

That's it. He was done making an ass of himself.

"I think it's time for me to head home," he said. "It's been a rough practice. I need about two hours in my whirlpool."

"I hear you. We're on our way out, too," Liani said.

"Can I give you two a ride somewhere?" he asked.

Chyna's eyes went wide with what could only be described as panic. "I…um…I think I forgot my cell phone back at the judging table," she said to Liani. "You go ahead. I'll see you tomorrow."

"I don't mind waiting," Jared offered.

"But I'm not going home. I told my mom I'd come over today. Just go on without me," she said, and took off down the hallway back toward the field house.

Jared pointed to Chyna's retreating form and turned to Liani. "Did I do that?" he asked.

Liani's grin spread from ear to ear. "I think you did. And all I can say is it's about time somebody got under her skin."

Chapter 3

As the doors closed at the Dekalb Station subway stop, Chyna inched closer to the back of the car. There would be a mass exodus at the Atlantic Avenue/Long Island Rail Road interchange and she had her eye on one of the seats toward the door. As soon as the train pulled to a stop, she shouldered her way to the back so she could get a seat before an incoming passenger could snatch it up.

She plopped onto the hard plastic and pulled her iPod from her duffel bag. Stuffing the ear buds in her ears, she skipped to Jennifer Lopez's "Love Don't Cost a Thing" and mentally rehearsed the routine she and Liani had put together for next season's opening preseason game. But before J.Lo could sing a note, Chyna pulled the ear buds out and, with an irritated sigh, stuffed the iPod back into her bag.

She needed to focus. This freelancing job Liani had helped her land with the Saberrettes was a golden opportunity. It was the first chance she'd been given to make some real money from her dancing. She needed to keep her head in the game. But concentrating on anything other than a certain unbelievably built football player just wasn't in the cards at the moment.

Jared Dawson had flirted with her. *Twice.*

Granted, he hadn't done the best job, but who was she to issue style points when it came to flirting? His very nearness had had her so discombobulated she had a hard time remembering either conversation.

That excuse she'd lobbed about adhering to the Saberrettes' rule against players and cheerleaders dating had been the most practical evasion tactic. Even though the rule didn't technically apply to her, witnessing the ramifications of Liani's encounter with one of the Sabers last year—her friend still refused to tell Chyna which one—had been enough of a deterrent. Chyna had enough things on her plate these days: school, her commitment to the dance studio where she volunteered, paying the bills, checking in on her folks. She certainly didn't need to add nursing a broken heart to the list.

Even if heartache wasn't the outcome of "engaging in some friendly conversation," as Jared had put it, Chyna simply didn't have time to get involved with anyone. Especially now that she was the official independent choreography consultant to the New York Saberrettes.

Her lips curved in a grin.

Independent choreography consultant. That had such a cool ring to it.

Despite the fact that the job was only temporary, and Lord knew the salary wouldn't have her yacht shopping anytime soon, this freelancing gig officially made her a professional dancer. She was earning money through dance. It was a start.

History had taught her better than to hang her hopes

on ever paying the bills with her love of dance, but that's why she wore uncomfortable high heels and worked hard every day as an administrative assistant. It was why she'd put herself through college, taking classes online for the past six years.

It was the reason she would eventually get that junior management position that had just been posted on the job board at the hedge fund where she'd worked since a week after high school graduation. She'd scraped her way up from errand girl to clerical assistant to senior administrative assistant. The junior management position required a college degree, which Chyna would have by the end of the summer semester.

That is, if she could get her mind off a certain football player long enough to concentrate on the ton of schoolwork she had to get done tonight.

Jared Dawson was supposed to be the safe crush. Liani had talked about how crazy in love he was with his girlfriend. Which was why, of all the Sabers players, he had been the most sensible candidate for lead role in Chyna's fantasies. She had never contemplated those fantasies becoming reality.

But after their second encounter of the day it was no longer a question. Jared wasn't interested in just making small talk.

Tingles of the very naughty variety skittered in places that had her blushing. Thank goodness for the relative indifference of New York subway riders. No one would notice her flustered state.

The disembodied voice announced the train's arrival at the Fort Hamilton station. Chyna lifted her duffel over her shoulder and exited the train. She walked four blocks to her building in Brooklyn's Bay Ridge neighborhood and made it up the two flights of stairs to her third-floor walk-up. She could hear her baby scratching at the door.

"Mommy's home, sweetie," Chyna called through the thick wood. She pushed the door open and was greeted by six pounds of excited dog prancing around her feet. Chyna dropped her duffel and her keys and scooped up her Yorkshire terrier, Summer, from the floor. "How is Mommy's baby? Mommy is so sorry she had to leave you alone all day."

She quickly grabbed Summer's leash and took her for a bladder-easing walk around the block. Back in her apartment, she filled Summer's doggie bowl, showered and heated up leftover pizza for dinner. Twenty minutes later, Chyna settled on the futon in her postage stamp-size living room that doubled as her office and dining room, and grabbed the stack of journal articles she'd gathered from the tomes of NYU's library.

Highlighter in hand, she read the same paragraph six times before tossing the article and highlighter aside. The frustrated growl she allowed herself didn't even begin to make her feel better. Not being able to concentrate on the Saberrettes' routine was one thing, but when thoughts of Jared got in the way of her schoolwork, it was a problem.

After six years of fitting in as many classes as her overstuffed schedule would allow, she was just a couple of months away from finally earning her college degree. Her academic future—no, scratch that—her *future,* period, depended on acing her independent study project.

Determined to put Jared and his endearingly bad attempts at flirting out of her mind, Chyna picked up the highlighter and forced herself to concentrate. She was good at compartmentalizing. Jared was a Saberrettes problem and since she'd left all things Saberrettes-related back at the Sabers facility, he was no longer an issue. For the rest of the night she would be Chyna McCrea, college student.

Summer scampered onto Chyna's lap. She plopped her chin on the journal article, her tiny ears perked up like antennas.

Chyna picked her up and rubbed her nose on her doggie's belly.

Make that Chyna McCrea, college student and doting mommy to one high-maintenance Yorkie.

Jared juggled three beers, a bag of Doritos and a bowl of peanut M&Ms from the bar in Torrian's tricked-out rec room. It occupied the basement of the four-story Murray Hill brownstone. The room had been gutted, then outfitted with a collection of toys that could make a grown man cry.

A mahogany pool table occupied one corner, while a trio of pinball machines and a virtual reality racing game took up another. In the middle of the far wall was a sweet seventy-inch LCD flat-panel television. Torrian had just had four smaller televisions—if you could call thirty-two-inch flat screens small—installed, one at each corner of the larger seventy inch screen.

Having a bevy of man toys at their fingertips was nice, but it was the marble gaming table that saw the most action. For the past four years the table had hosted countless games of dominoes, with the occasional poker game thrown in to change up the pace.

Thank God for game night. After the whirlwind of changes he'd been through since walking in on Samantha and Carlos, Jared was infinitely grateful for this dose of familiarity.

Theo Stokes, former linebacker for the Sabers who now worked as a commentator for the all-sports network

Sports Talk TV, shuffled the dominoes around on the table. "You said Paige is at a blogger's convention?" he asked Torrian.

"Yeah, don't ask me what bloggers have to convene about. Don't ask her, either. It'll get you slapped."

Jared grinned. "Thanks for the warning. Of course, that's the first thing I'm going to ask the next time I see her."

Torrian's fiancée, Paige Turner, was a former blogger for an entertainment magazine. She'd given up her position to become the PR person for Torrian's restaurant, the Fire Starter Grille, and had recently started up a new blog dedicated solely to dining out in New York City.

Jared grabbed a handful of Doritos. "Are we ever going to have Deirdre's cooking again?" he asked before stuffing the chips into his mouth.

"Did I hear my name?" came a voice from the top of the stairs. Torrian's sister, Deirdre Smallwood, head chef at the Fire Starter Grille, started down the stairs carrying a tray.

"I had a couple of these mini empanadas left over from today," she said when she reached the landing. She headed straight for the side table, setting the tray on it.

"Thank God. I miss having you spoil us, Dee." Jared rose from his chair to give her a peck on the cheek.

"I figure you boys are grown now, but a little spoiling never hurts." She laughed then returned his kiss. She turned to the table, faltering a step. "Hello, Thelonious," she directed at Theo, who responded with one curt nod, and a very brisk, "Deirdre."

Jared looked from one to the other as he slid back in his chair. The tension between them was so thick he doubted one of Deirdre's sharp chef knives could slice through it. Jared glanced over at Torrian, who shook his head and made a cutting motion at his neck.

Okay. Something was definitely going on there.

"Well," Deirdre said, clasping her hands together. "I guess I'll see you all later. Torrian, don't forget, you promised to pick Dante up from his friend's house. I don't want him riding the subway after what happened last Friday night."

"I'm on it," Torrian said.

They were quiet as Deirdre walked up the stairs. As soon as the door closed behind her, all three men at the table spoke at once.

"What happened with Dante?" Theo asked Torrian.

"Why are you such a jackass?" Torrian spat at Theo.

"What's going on between you two?" Jared questioned.

Theo held up a hand. "Answer my question first. What happened with Dante last Friday night?" he asked, referring to Torrian's seventeen-year-old nephew.

"He got jumped on the train heading out of Brooklyn."

"Is he okay?" Theo asked.

"He was a little roughed up. Nothing too bad. Deirdre's more worked up about it than Dante. I'm surprised she let him go out at all."

"What do you expect?" Jared chimed in. "He's her only child. Of course she's going to be overprotective."

Torrian turned to Theo. "Now answer my question. Is there a reason you automatically turn into a jerk whenever Deirdre is around?"

"He's scared of her," Jared said.

"Shut up," Theo barked.

"Admit it, dawg. You don't know what the heck you're doing when it comes to Dee." Torrian pointed a finger at him. "I'm warning you. If you wait too long to figure it out, you're going to miss your chance."

"Are we gonna play dominoes or gossip like a bunch of girls?" Theo growled.

"Can't we do both?"

The look Theo shot Torrian's way was pure evil. Jared decided to step in to prevent possible bloodshed.

"If it'll make you feel better, you're not the only one with woman troubles." His friends both looked at him with uneasy stares. "I'm not talking about the obvious," Jared said. "I told you all I'm over Samantha. For the most part," he tacked on at the end.

"About time," Theo drawled.

"In my attempt to put Sam behind me, I tried to make a move on someone else today. I got shot down hard."

"Oh, yeah, you owe me this story." Torrian chuckled. He glanced over at Theo and nodded toward Jared. "This one decided to go after one of the Saberrettes."

"Dude, seriously?" Theo laughed.

"She's not a Saberrette," Jared clarified. "She's a choreographer the squad hired to help with new routines for next season. It doesn't matter one way or the other. She wouldn't cut me a bit of slack." Jared shook his head, laughing at himself. "I felt like a fool. I'm so out of practice with this stuff."

"Look, if you want to get her attention—" Theo started, but Torrian stopped him.

"Hold up! *You* are trying to give woman advice? You?"

"Just because you tricked Paige into giving you the time of day doesn't make you Casanova."

"Casanova had dozens of women, not just one. Shows how much you know."

Jared settled back in his chair to enjoy the show as two of his best friends volleyed insults back and forth at each other. But it didn't take long for him to tune them both out, his mind conjuring an image of heavenly gray eyes in a face fit for an angel. God, she was lovely.

Whether she admitted it or not there was definitely chemistry between them. Jared saw it in the way her smile had softened when she looked at him. It was only after the threat of being confined in a car with him that she'd panicked. He decided to take that as a good sign.

Theo and Torrian were still trying to decide who was better equipped to give woman advice. Jared didn't have the heart to tell them he didn't need their help. He knew what he was going to do as far as Chyna was concerned.

He was going to win her over.

She'd thrown down the gauntlet when she'd scurried away from him earlier today. If there was one thing Jared loved, it was a good competition. Even better, he loved to win. His competitive nature was the foundation of everything he did. It was why he loved the game of football so much. It was why gambling had grabbed him by the throat. That very first win at the craps table had been all he had needed to become hooked.

Today, Chyna had pulled at the competitive cord that ran through his veins. She was a challenge. A very *hot* challenge who made him feel things he thought would take months, if not years, to feel again. And like every other challenge he'd faced, he was determined to come out on top. One way or another, he was going to win her over.

Jared shook his head, a rueful grin tipping up his lips. As much as he hated to admit it, Randall was right. A summer fling was just the kind of diversion he needed.

And if his teammate's claim about Chyna was true, she needed him to distract her from her hectic life just as much as Jared needed her to help rid his mind of Samantha.

She was too young, too vibrant, too beautiful to be so serious. She needed someone to show her how to cut loose and have a good time.

His grin growing wider, Jared decided he was just the man for the job.

Chapter 4

"Congratulations on making the squad." Chyna shook the hand of the final new addition to the Saberrettes squad, then returned to the judges' table to gather up the score sheets that littered the surface.

"Hey." Liani sidled up next to her. She wrapped an arm around Chyna's shoulder. "A couple of us are taking the new girls out for margaritas. You in?"

"Sounds like fun, but I can't," Chyna said. "I've got work to do."

"You always have work to do," Liani lamented. "Why don't you stop being a grown-up for a few hours and have some fun? Work can wait."

"It can't. I'm working on my independent study project. You know that."

"Oh, just do like everyone else does and pay someone to write it."

"I've been trying to teach Summer how to do my

research, but she just can't seem to grasp it. Yorkies have such short attention spans."

Liani rolled her eyes. "Whatever."

"You all can join me at the Patisserie if you'd like. Scones, coffee and hours of reading academic journals. Tell me that doesn't sound like fun."

"You are such a party animal," Liani said with the enthusiasm of a rock.

"I'll talk to you later." Chyna laughed. "Remember, you promised we'd have a girls' night soon."

"I'm not the one who's canceled twice already," Liani called over her shoulder as she rejoined the other squad members still milling about.

Chyna swallowed the bitter pill of guilt. More often than not she was the one who had to back out when she and her best friend had plans. It wasn't her fault there were only twenty-four hours in a day. With all the things crowding her plate, socializing was usually the first to take a backseat.

She quickly packed up her gear, determined to make it to the Patisserie before the Sunday afternoon crowd descended on it. Ever since some food blogger featured it in an article about the best bakeries in each borough, Chyna's favorite study place had been overrun by strangers.

She waved goodbye to the girls that still remained as she left the field house and headed for the exit. At least she hoped she was heading for the exit. Although she had been working with the dance squad for several weeks now, she still felt as if she needed a GPS system to navigate her way through the Sabers' massive state-of-the-art practice compound.

Chyna's heart engaged in a little pitter-patter action as she entered the hallway that led to the compound's front lobby. Just the thought of running into a certain member of the team had tendrils of excitement skittering along her skin. She'd caught a few glimpses of Jared today, but he hadn't spent much time on the indoor practice field.

She had to keep reminding herself that she did *not* want to see him. Included in the social aspect of life that she just didn't have time for were men in general, much to Liani's discontent. Never mind the fact that her friend had begged off men after last season's incident with that unnamed Saber, Liani still harped on Chyna's assertion that, in the grand scheme of things, being in a relationship held little appeal these days. Relationships took time, something Chyna could not afford to give to someone else right now.

Still, a nice dinner and some friendly conversation couldn't hurt.

Wait. Where had that come from?

Chyna didn't have to toil too long to remember. The idea of *friendly* conversation had been on her mind way too much since a certain someone had suggested it yesterday.

She *so* could not allow Jared Dawson and all his yumminess to put ideas into her head. Getting involved with someone, even on a casual level, was not a part of her game plan. Finish school, get the job promotion and start saving for a down payment on her own dance studio. *That* was the plan. She didn't have time for obsessing over Jared.

If only those memories of the way that T-shirt had stretched across his ripped chest didn't make her heart beat faster than a solid hour of dance practice.

God, she was in *such* trouble.

As she came upon an intersection in the facility's main building, a door to her right opened and several people filed out. Apparently, fate was in a taunting mood today, because Jared emerged just as Chyna passed the door. She quickened her steps, power walking down the hallway toward the main exit doors.

"Hey, Chyna. Wait a minute."

She ignored him as she moved swiftly across the lobby and charged through the double doors, feeling like a complete and utter fool. Had she actually run from the man?

Yes. *Hell, yes.*

As she made her way to the train station, Chyna revisited all the reasons that running from Jared and those butterflies he set off in her stomach was the absolute smartest thing she could do. She made it home with just enough time to feed and walk Summer before heading to the Patisserie. She decided to forgive fate for that run-in with Jared when she walked into the bakery and found her favorite chair unoccupied.

Chyna settled in with an espresso, a flaky croissant and the journal articles she should have finished reading the night before. The parade of newcomers had started their invasion, but Chyna did her best to tune them out. Before she knew it, an hour had passed and she'd gotten through two of the five articles.

She left the comfy confines of the well-worn leather chair just long enough to get another espresso. By sheer willpower she passed on a second pastry. Settling back into her chair, Chyna brought the demitasse to her lips just as the bell above the bakery's entrance clanged a delicate chime. She looked up and nearly spit coffee all over herself.

Standing in the doorway was Jared Dawson.

Even before the mouthwatering aroma of the pastries hit him, Jared was smacked with an awareness of Chyna.

His eyes zeroed in directly on the spot she occupied along the bakery's rear wall. She stared back at him, the tiny cup in her hand arrested midair. Jared bypassed the food display and headed straight for her.

She was fumbling with a stack of papers in her lap. She looked up at him and stole the breath from his lungs.

She wore glasses. The thin wire frames were the same gray as her eyes, which were even more luminous behind the lenses. Jared knew he should say something, but words failed him. He was content to just stare at her.

Apparently, she wasn't.

"What are you doing here?" she asked, the question laced with puzzlement and a touch of annoyance.

"Would you believe I just happened to be in the neighborhood?"

"No," she answered without hesitation.

"Guilty as charged," he admitted with a smirk. He looked around and spotted an empty chair at a table a few feet away. He asked the couple seated there if he could borrow it, signed a quick autograph for the guy who happened to be a Sabers fan—surprise, surprise—then sat the chair just to Chyna's right.

As he lowered onto the chair, his right knee brushed against her thigh and the jolt of sensation was the first indication that he was in trouble. The second was the tightening in his groin when she turned those amazing eyes on him again.

"How did you know I would be here?" she asked, then answered her own question, growling her friend's name. "Liani."

"She didn't give you up easily. It cost me an autographed jersey for her nephew, but it was worth it."

"Why is that? Especially when I already told you I'm not interested?"

"Because I don't believe you," Jared said. "The look on your face when I walked through that door back there didn't look like disinterest to me, Chyna. In fact, it was the complete opposite." When she didn't respond, he continued. "Tell me you're not the slightest bit intrigued by this chemistry we seem to have."

"Chemistry?" She choked on a laugh. But it wasn't a humorous laugh; it was a nervous one, which confirmed exactly what Jared had been thinking since the minute he'd spoken to her yesterday. She felt this. Damn right, she felt it.

Recovering, she gestured to the space that separated them. "You think there's chemistry here?"

Jared closed the space even more, until he was only inches from her face. "Absolutely," he murmured, his eyes zeroing in on her lips. They trembled slightly, and she pulled the bottom one between her teeth. That sliver of vulnerability hit him like a gut punch. "Tell me, Chyna," Jared softly challenged. "Tell me you don't feel this."

"Fine," she said on a shaky breath. "I feel it." Then she shook her head, seeming to have broken the spell that had wrapped around them both. Stiffening her spine, she picked up that tiny coffee cup and took an even tinier sip. "So, I admit that there's something going on here. Whether it's chemistry or the type of mushrooms Gianni's used on my pizza last night, I can't be sure."

"I didn't have psychedelic mushrooms last night." Jared grinned. "Try again."

"You know what? This chemistry thing doesn't even matter because I'm still not interested."

"What if I am?" he threw back at her.

"Why would you be?"

Jared barked out a laugh. "Is that a real question?" he asked.

Did he *really* have to explain why just the thought of her set his blood on high boil? He wasn't sure he could put it into words, because he had yet to explain it to himself. Was it because she'd turned him down? His hate-to-lose attitude probably had something to do with it, but this thing he was feeling went beyond the superficial.

There was something about Chyna that fascinated him. The contradiction she presented sitting here with a pile of work in her lap made him question just who was hiding behind those studious glasses. Was the carefree professional choreographer masquerading as an intellectual, or was it the other way around?

He couldn't let go of what Randall had said about her. His teammate had called her boring, but Jared had a hard time accepting that description. A dull, boring woman wouldn't make his blood pressure spike.

No, Chyna wasn't boring. Overwhelmed, maybe. Exhaustion was written all over her face. And from the mountain of paperwork surrounding her, it looked as if she was in for a long night.

If he could help her forget, just for an hour, about whatever had those pretty gray eyes clouding with unease, Jared would feel as if he'd accomplished something. The force of this need to alleviate her troubles stunned him, but he couldn't deny it. He was determined to put a smile on Chyna's face.

"I know how to solve this," Chyna said, pushing her glasses higher on her nose and crossing her arms over her chest. "What if I told you there was not a chance that I would sleep with you?"

A grin spread across Jared's lips. Oh, yeah, she was definitely scared of what he made her feel. He hadn't said a thing about them sleeping together. *Yet.* They hadn't even had a first date. Though he would remedy that soon enough.

He gave her a nonchalant shrug. "I'd say it's no big deal. I've gotten pretty use to cold showers."

"Oh, please." She looked at him with such disbelief, Jared couldn't help but chuckle.

"Do you really think the only reason I came here was to get you to sleep with me?" He bent forward, and in a staged whisper, said, "Believe it or not, if that's all I was interested in, I had a lot of options, and none of them would have cost me a jersey or a drive to Brooklyn."

"So why did you come here?" she asked.

Jared stared at that breathtaking face, completely mesmerized. "I've asked myself that about a hundred times since Liani told me where to find you. I thought maybe you could help me figure it out."

She didn't speak, just continued to stare at him with those eyes he could easily drown in. Jared didn't know how much time passed, but with every second he found himself sinking deeper and deeper.

What was it about her that had reached in and grabbed hold of him? It was unnerving. Scary, even. The last woman who'd affected him this quickly had held his heart for ten years. And then she'd crushed it.

He wouldn't do that to himself again. Not this soon. Not ever.

Yet as he gazed into the smoky depths of Chyna's captivating stare, Jared feared it was already out of his control. Before she could say another word he leaned in closer and said in an almost desperate plea, "Have dinner with me. Please," he added. His heart beat like a brass band within his chest as he awaited her answer.

She shook her head. "That's not a good idea."

"It's just dinner, Chyna. That's all I want."

"No, it's not."

Jared couldn't help the rueful grin that hitched up a corner of his mouth. "Okay, so it's not the only thing I want, but it's all I'm asking for. A couple of hours of some conversation over a good meal. That's not too much to ask, is it?"

Say yes, Jared silently pleaded. He could see the indecision in her stormy eyes. She wanted to say yes, Jared felt it in his bones. But something was holding her back. "I can't date Sabers players," she maintained.

"Forget that I'm a Saber. That's my job, but it's not who I am." He took the risk of reaching for her hand. "It's not number forty-two of the New York Sabers who wants to have dinner with you. It's just me. Jared."

She stared at their joined hands for long moments, the silence stretching between them. When she titled her head up, her answer was there in her eyes. Jared's shoulders slumped with relief before she even had the chance to reward him with her wry smile.

"Fine," she said with a resigned sigh. "I'll have dinner with you."

Chapter 5

"Chyna, do you have the commodities report?"

Chyna looked up from her computer screen to find Eric Steinberg peering over the top of her cubicle.

"It's still printing," she answered. She snatched the papers from the bed of her printer and tapped them on the desk, straightening the thirty-plus-page report that would likely be skimmed then tossed aside. The printer spit out the last couple of pages, and Chyna added them to the stack and handed it to Eric across the top of the five feet high cubicle wall.

"Hey," Eric whispered. "Meet me in the copy room in five minutes."

"You're a newlywed, Eric. You shouldn't be inviting coworkers to the copy room," Chyna said, tsking.

He cut her with a dirty look. "Just meet me in the copy room."

Grinning, Chyna locked her computer screen and headed for the common area. She peeked into several of her coworkers' workspaces as she traveled along the long corridor of cubicles.

"Thanks for your help with the commodities report, Elaine. I just turned it in," she said to one of the interns who shared a cubicle with two others.

Chyna remembered those days. When she'd first started at Marlowe & Brown Hedge Fund eight years ago, not only did she share a cubicle with two other girls, they all shared the same computer. She'd graduated to a computer of her own several months later and over the course of the past eight years had moved to her own cubicle.

But she had her eyes on a bigger prize. An office. With a door. And, be still her heart, possibly even a window.

Okay, that was asking for a bit too much. She would be happy to work in a space where coworkers had to knock to enter instead of just poking their heads over the top of her cubicle. Chyna was so close she could taste the free lattes that were served in the Monday morning management meetings.

She entered the kitchen and poured herself a cup of coffee—not a fancy latte, but a caffeine boost nonetheless. She was emptying a packet of sweetener into her cup when Eric's voice jolted her.

"I said the copy room," he said.

She jumped, sending sweetener everywhere. "Goodness, Eric!" Chyna dusted at the smattering of white powder that clung to the front of her sweater. "If you don't mind, I'd prefer not to have a heart attack today."

Eric grabbed her by the elbow and pulled her out of the open kitchen area and into the adjacent copy room where he closed the door.

"What's so urgent?" Chyna asked, wringing her arm from his grip.

"Guess who just accepted a job with the Cohen Group?" Eric asked with a smug grin.

"You're leaving?"

"Not me," Eric snorted. "Are you forgetting who my father-in-law is? I'm here for life."

"Then who?" Chyna asked.

"Katie Parker."

Her heart started thumping like a Broadway ensemble within her chest. "Don't you toy with me, Eric Steinberg."

"Being the son-in-law of one of the founding partners has its perks," Eric said. "Melissa and I had dinner at her folks' place last night. Tom spent the entire meal griping about the Cohen Group stealing away his employees. He said Katie turned in her resignation yesterday afternoon."

Chyna managed to quell the exhilaration that was on the verge of erupting out of her, but just barely. There were several candidates vying for the recently vacated junior management position in Marlowe & Brown's Risk Assessment department, but Katie Parker was the only one with an edge over Chyna. Katie had recently earned a MBA in finance whereas Chyna was still working on her bachelor's degree. They had both been at the hedge fund for eight years and were even when it came to practical work experience. And they were both light years ahead of the other candidates.

If Katie was no longer in the running for the position…

"Eric, are you one hundred percent sure about this?" Chyna asked. "You'd better not be toying with me."

"I'd never joke about something like this. She's leaving at the end of March," Eric said. "That job is yours. Congratulations." He gave her a thumbs-up before heading out of the copy room.

Chyna sucked in a steadying breath, hoping to abate the excited, almost nauseated feeling stirring in the pit of her stomach.

This was what she wanted. It was what she'd been working toward for the past eight years. When she'd applied for a job as the assistant to an assistant at Marlowe & Brown, she hadn't even known what a hedge fund was. Three weeks out of high school, the only thing she'd known was that she wanted to work somewhere that required a business suit. She used to envy the women in suits who had always looked so important riding the subway on their way into the city. Her goal in life had been to become one of them.

It hadn't taken her long to discover that at a place like Marlowe & Brown, even the coffee fetchers were required to wear business suits, which was why she'd devised her five-year plan. It had taken Chyna longer than she'd first anticipated—she'd had to take off two semesters from school when her dad first fell ill. But it had all been worth it in the end. She was less than a semester away from earning her bachelor's degree, the only requirement of the junior management position that she did not possess. If Katie Parker and her MBA were no longer a threat, that job was hers.

Chyna told herself the burning in her chest was just a touch of indigestion from the overly strong coffee, and not uneasiness. She straightened the tiny boxes of paper clips and Post-it notes in the supply cabinet. Now that the prize was within her grasp, she needed a few moments to digest this new turn of events and think about how it would affect her life.

She needed this promotion. The salary was nearly

forty percent more than what she was currently making as an administrative assistant. Of course, it also meant she would no longer be a nonexempt employee, but that didn't matter. She was hardly ever called on to work overtime.

That would change if she moved into the junior management position, though. Chyna had worked in Risk Assessment long enough to know the ins and outs of the department. It was commonplace to find management here long after the sun had gone down.

What would she do about the classes she taught at the dance school three times a week? Her girls wouldn't understand anything about reviewing and analyzing credit inquiries. The only thing they would understand was that their teacher had pushed them to the side because she had more important things to do.

"You don't even have the job yet," Chyna chastised herself under her breath. Liani constantly accused her of heaping unnecessary worry on her head. She was beginning to see her friend's point.

Still, as she made her way back to her cubicle, Chyna couldn't help but think about all she would have to give up in order to earn an office with a door. She had devised a pros-versus-cons list the minute she'd learned of the position, and even though the cons were winning by a landslide, there was one thing on the pros list that outweighed everything else.

Security.

This promotion would mean having a savings account that could finally reach five figures before she had to dip into it to help her parents out with their bills during the months when their fixed income couldn't cover them all. It would mean having the freedom to buy herself a nice sweater or pair of shoes without waiting for them to go on sale.

Chyna didn't want to think about the things she would have to give up if she were offered this new job. Nothing was as essential as the peace of mind that would come with her forty-percent-bigger paycheck.

She sat behind her desk and pulled up another report that was due by the end of the day. Her cell phone trilled in her purse.

"That's the third time in less than twenty minutes your phone has rung," her coworker Ma Ling said from one cubicle over.

Chyna's breath caught. That many calls in such a short time span could only mean one thing: something had happened to her dad. She dove into the bag for the phone, imagining her dad on a stretcher with an oxygen mask over his face.

She didn't recognize the number. Oh, God, it had to be a hospital calling.

Ma Ling stood just outside the entrance to her cubicle, concern pinching her forehead into a pronounced vee.

"What happened?" Chyna answered with a frantic gasp.

"Is that how you answer the phone?"

Jared Dawson's amused murmur sent a barrage of emotions ping-ponging through Chyna's system. Relief that it wasn't the hospital calling to say her dad had finally coughed up one of his emphysemic lungs was instantaneously followed by a surge of nervous energy.

"Sorry," she said. "I thought it was some kind of an emergency."

"It is, in a way. I only have five minutes left of my break before another two hours of drills. I wanted to make sure I got hold of you before going back to the practice field."

Chyna eyed her coworker standing anxiously a few feet away. She covered the receiver and mouthed, "It's okay."

Ma Ling's tense face visibly relaxed and she returned to her cubicle.

"Are you still there?" Jared asked.

"I am," Chyna said, pushing away from her desk. "Just…give me a minute."

The cubicles didn't offer much privacy, and she didn't want the entire office to know that Jared Dawson was on the other end of the line. The minute she'd shared news of her freelancing job with the Saberrettes, her coworkers had started bombarding her with questions about the team, despite Chyna's repeated insistence that she did not have unlimited access to Sabers players. If anyone found out it was Jared on the phone the questions would never stop.

Chyna made it to the restroom and dipped inside. She stooped low, checking for feet under the stalls.

"Chyna?"

"I'm here," she said. "Just making sure I'm alone. Jared, why are you calling me?" she asked, though she already knew the answer.

"To find out what time I should pick you up tonight," he replied.

Chyna's eyelids slid shut. She'd been holding on to a string of hope that he'd forgotten about the dinner date she'd agreed to in the one moment her common sense had decided to go on vacation. She knew she should have called and canceled, but between work, class and the dozens of other things on her plate, time had slipped away from her.

"Jared. I'm sorry, but I can't go out with you tonight."

"Did something come up?"

Yeah. Her good sense. "You can say that," Chyna said.

"What about tomorrow night?"

She should just come out with it. She had always been a Band-Aid ripper, not the gently tug type.

"Not tomorrow, either. I can't go out with you. At all."

"Why?" The one-word question was drenched in disappointment.

Chyna winced. What had she been thinking to agree to a date with him in the first place? "I told you before, there are rules against dating players."

"Haven't we already discussed this? That rule doesn't apply to you since you're not an official member of the squad."

"Call it a personal rule then. I don't go out with Sabers players." He groaned on the other side of the phone line. "I didn't say my rule was fair, but it's still my rule," Chyna said.

"Well, I think you should have an exception."

"It was Cedric Reeves, but I heard he's off the market," she teased, hoping to lessen the blow of her refusal. That she was concerned about his feelings at all sounded alarm bells ringing in her head. His feelings, hurt or otherwise, had nothing to do with her.

"That's not funny," Jared said about her quip. "Honestly, Chyna, are ball players really so bad?"

"Not all of you," she said. "It has more to do with me. I—" The bathroom door opened and a woman from the acquisitions division entered. Chyna lowered her voice. "It's not you," she said.

"You didn't just try to feed me the 'It's not you, it's me' line, did you?"

She totally had. How guys who used that line could

stomach the overwhelming sense of smarminess that engulfed her was mind-boggling.

"In this instance, it fits," she stated. "Look, Jared, I really need to get back to work. I'm sorry if you made plans already, but you'll need to cancel them. Or just take one of the other girls from the squad," she finished, then ended the call before he could respond.

Chyna braced her hands against the countertop and studied her reflection in the mirror. Canceling had been the smart thing to do.

Liani had filled her in on how things worked between the players and those cheerleaders who chose to break the no-fraternizing rule. The girls allowed themselves to be wined and dined as they played the part of the hot girlfriend. Sometimes they got a pair of nice earrings or the latest Coach bag out of the deal, but often it was at the price of their self-respect.

The thought of finding herself in that same position ate at the very core of her being. She didn't need to latch on to a rich football player to get by in life. She had learned to rely on herself a long time ago. Ever since the day her father lashed out at her for asking for money to attend dance classes, Chyna recognized that if she wanted something she had to get it for herself. She'd collected aluminum cans and did odd jobs for her neighbors until she'd earned enough money to send herself to dance camp.

She didn't need anyone to take care of her. She did just fine on her own.

Jared had seemed sincere when he'd interrupted her study session last Sunday night. In fact, he'd been so sweet that she was hit with the warm fuzzies every time she walked passed the Patisserie, and it had nothing to do with their chocolate-filled croissants.

But it didn't matter. She had papers to write and dance classes to teach. She had a job promotion to score. She didn't have time in her life for any man right now, and even if she did, it wouldn't be a member of the New York Sabers.

When the clock hit four o'clock, the only thing Chyna had left to do was log out of her computer. Today had been, in a word, exhausting. As she passed the management team's offices on her way out of the Risk Assessment wing, she managed to taper the excited tingle that started in her belly. She would be one of them soon.

But as she continued down the corridor, a slight tremor of unease flitted within the walls of Chyna's chest. Not a single one of those people looked even remotely ready to head home for the day. Was this her future?

Chyna tossed the thought out of her head. She didn't want to jinx herself. If the job was meant to be hers, it would be, and she would handle it the way she'd handled everything else that had been thrown at her in life.

She exited the side door of the office building and headed up Seventh Avenue. When she turned the corner at Thirty-fourth Street, Jared was standing a few feet away, at the building's main entrance.

He spotted her, and the most delicious smile stretched across his face.

Chyna crossed her arms over her chest and shook her head. "Liani Dixon, the friendship was nice while it lasted, but I'm afraid I'll have to kill you," she said to no one in particular.

"Don't blame Liani this time." Jared laughed. "Blame Google. Someone posted a picture of you at some fancy banquet and it listed you as an employee at Marlowe and Brown."

"I can't believe you searched for me on the internet," she said.

"I can't believe you were going to stand me up tonight," he returned.

"I'm still going to stand you up." She made a move to walk past him, but he captured her elbow.

"Why?" he asked. "And don't feed me that stuff about you not dating football players."

She stared into his eyes. They were the loveliest shade of brown—almost hazel. "Why do I have to give you a reason at all?" Chyna asked in a voice she hardly recognized as her own.

"Because you owe me at least that much for suggesting I just take out one of the other girls. What was that about?"

His wounded, accusatory tone stung. "I'm sorry," Chyna said. "That was thoughtless. But I still don't owe you a reason for refusing to have dinner with you."

"What's the harm, Chyna? You do plan to eat tonight, don't you?"

"Don't pretend it's that simple," she reproved. "We both know my agreeing to dinner would mean more than just sharing a meal."

"Yes, it would mean treating yourself to some downtime. Take a few hours to just kick back and enjoy yourself." He took a step closer, a flash of heat flaring in his steady gaze. "I'm not bad company, Chyna. Why don't you give me a shot?"

She wavered slightly, tormented by the confusing emotions volleying back and forth in her head. She thought back to when she'd first met him at the Sabers compound. Despite his horrible attempts at flirting, there had been a certain charm. And the fact that he'd been interested enough to seek her out later that day had to account for something, didn't it?

Allowing herself a couple of hours for a nice dinner wouldn't cause her entire schedule to crumble. She could spare just this one night, couldn't she?

"Okay," Chyna finally answered. "Meet me at the Patisserie at seven-thirty."

"Can't I pick you up at your place?"

"No," she said. "The bakery is fine."

A delectable smile curved up one corner of his mouth. "You promise not to stand me up?"

"Promise," she said.

For a moment, Chyna thought he would kiss her. Instead, he trailed his finger across her jaw in a gentle caress, turned and headed the opposite way up Thirty-fourth. She wasn't sure how long she stood in the middle of the sidewalk while hundreds of New Yorkers rushed passed her. Only one thought occupied her mind.

What in the heck had she just gotten herself into?

Jared pulled the silk sheets from his California king-size bed and stuffed them in the hamper in his closet. Normally, he'd leave this for Maggie, his housekeeper, to deal with, but when she'd left his condo yesterday she'd mentioned having to take care of three grandkids all suffering with a stomach virus. Jared figured she'd need a break.

Besides, stripping the bedding gave him something to do. He still had two and a half hours until his date with Chyna.

Was he seriously counting down the hours?

Jared shook his head, grinning at himself. It was better than how he'd spent the past dozen Friday nights, sitting in this apartment alone, trying not to think about what he could have been doing if things hadn't ended with Samantha. Talk about a surefire way to send him on a first-class trip to his own personal hell.

Jared's gaze drifted to the bed they'd shared. His jaw tightened as he remembered the way she would snuggle up next to him. Had it all been a lie? All those years he'd spent giving her everything she could ever ask for. Could it really have meant nothing?

He tore his eyes away from the bed. Why he hadn't pitched the damn thing to the curb was a question he didn't have the energy to explore. Maybe Torrian was right when he'd accused him of being into self-torture. Maybe he'd always been a sadomasochist and was just now figuring it out.

Jared let out a vicious curse. He was done with today's half-assed attempt at psychoanalysis. He refused to surrender another second of his life to *what might have been*. Tonight was a huge step in his mission to get over Samantha, and as far as diversions went, Chyna McCrea would definitely fit the bill.

With renewed resolve, Jared marched over to his cavernous walk-in closet. He pulled out the dark brown slacks Maggie had brought in from the dry cleaners and laid them across his valet. He hadn't settled on which jacket to pair with them. It all depended on where he took Chyna tonight.

He was waiting to hear from his friend Rena at Per Se, one of the most exclusive restaurants in Manhattan. He'd played the Sabers card, but even that wasn't a guarantee at the restaurant that was booked up months in advance. If Per Se fell through, he always had the Fire Starter Grille as a backup plan. Torrian had special tables for fellow Sabers personnel.

Jared heard movement coming from the kitchen.

Moments later, Maggie's soft knock sounded on his bedroom door.

"Mr. Dawson?"

"In here," Jared called. "And if you don't stop calling me Mr. Dawson, you're fired."

She waved off his threat. "Oh, Mr. Dawson." Four years and the woman still refused to call him by his first name. "I'll have your protein shake ready in a few minutes," she said, taking the dark brown jacket he'd been mulling over from his hands and replacing it with a bone-colored Oscar de la Renta.

"Much better choice." Jared nodded. "Don't worry about making dinner tonight. I have a date."

Maggie's head popped up from the laundry she'd begun sorting through. "With Ms. Miller?" she asked.

"No, not Sam," he said.

"Thank God," she breathed.

"Tell me how you really feel," Jared snorted.

Maggie crumpled the sweatpants in her hands, a sad smile on her round, peach-colored face. "I know it is not my place to say anything, Mr. Dawson, but I've been worried about you ever since she left. You haven't been yourself."

"I know, but I'm fine now. Really," he said when Maggie raised a skeptical brow. "Besides, I don't pay you enough to worry about me," he teased. They both knew it was a joke. He paid Maggie a generous salary, so generous that he'd become her sole client.

"You need to have someone to worry over you for a change," Maggie said. "And now that my youngest boy has left for college, it frees up space in my worry bank. Now, out of my way so I can get these in the wash and mix up your shake."

Having been dismissed from his bedroom, Jared

ambled around the apartment, trying to figure out what to do with himself for the next two hours. He plopped down in front of his iMac and tried catching up on what the sports bloggers were saying about the Sabers' upcoming Organized Team Activities, but there was nothing more than the usual chatter. There wouldn't be much to say until the off-season OTAs actually began in a couple of weeks.

His cell phone rang just as he was pushing away from the computer. Jared frowned at the unfamiliar number.

"Dawson," he answered.

"Hello, Mr. Dawson, this is Jackson Phillips from Fidelity Bank and Trust. I'm calling about your business loan."

"Dammit," Jared cursed. He'd forgotten about signing the papers for the Red Zone, the high-end, sports-themed barbershop venture he'd entered into with one of his old college buddies. "We had a four o'clock appointment, didn't we?"

"Yes," the man said. "Your business partner was here this morning. Your signature is the only thing that's needed to close."

"Yeah, I know." *Dammit.* It was just after five o'clock. Even though the bank wasn't far, getting there and back would be pushing it, especially since he still had to shower, dress and get all the way to Brooklyn before seven.

But he had to get those papers signed before the weekend. The grand opening of the Red Zone was next week. If the bank didn't sign off on the loan, the city couldn't go through with the final inspection and the building might not be ready in time. Patrick was counting on him.

Dammit!

"I can be there in a half hour," Jared said, leaving his

office and heading for his bedroom. "Can I meet you at six?"

"The bank usually closes at six, but for you I'll make an exception."

Jared thanked him as he declined the protein shake Maggie tried to hand him on his way to the master suite. He jumped in the shower and was out of his apartment less than twenty minutes after receiving the call from the bank. Jared walked out of the building and groaned at the bumper-to-bumper traffic clogging the street. It would be a miracle if he made it to the bank by six o'clock.

On the bright side, by the time he was done crisscrossing downtown Manhattan, he'd have only a few minutes before it was time to pick up Chyna.

Chapter 6

"No." Liani snatched the black slacks from Chyna's grasp and pivoted, staring into the open closet.

"What was wrong with those?" Chyna lamented.

Liani glared at her with annoyance usually reserved for parents chastising a recalcitrant child.

"You are going out with Jared Dawson," her friend said. "You need to think sexy, and pants are not sexy." Liani gestured to Chyna's lower half. "You are five foot eight with a pair of the most incredible legs I've ever seen. Show them off."

Chyna flashed her a flirtatious smile. "You've been checking out my legs?"

Liani practically growled. "Stop playing around and pick a dress. I have to leave in a half hour, and it'll take at least that long to do your hair and makeup."

Chyna settled on her favorite little black dress. It was sleeveless with a scooping neckline, practical but elegant. "I don't want to go over the top," she reasoned. "I'm not even sure where we're going. We may decide to just stay at the Patisserie and have paninis."

"This is Jared Dawson we're talking about," Liani stressed unnecessarily. As if Chyna needed a reminder of whom she would be meeting in just under an hour. "He is *not* going to take you to a coffee shop for sandwiches. Jared doesn't skimp. I've told you stories of how he doted on that stupid girlfriend of his."

"Well, I'm not stupid and I'm not his girlfriend," Chyna pointed out. She sat in front of the mirror and waited for Liani, who was retrieving makeup from a collection that would make the girls at the Sephora counter seethe with envy. "It's not as if this is anything serious," Chyna continued. "The only reason I'm going out with him is because I knew he wouldn't stop asking until I caved."

Liar.

Liani looked up from the cosmetic case and shot her a look that said she was wholly unconvinced.

"Okay, fine. I also think he's just a bit gorgeous, too," Chyna conceded.

"Thank God. I was about to question your sanity. Turn toward me." Liani caught Chyna's chin between her fingers. "Actually, I still think you're crazy," she muttered through thinned lips as she drew a thin black line along the lower lash of Chyna's eye. "If Jared Dawson was in hot pursuit, I would be all too ready to let him catch me."

"I don't have time to get caught," Chyna complained. This conversation was starting to sound like a broken record. No matter how many times she stated her case, Liani couldn't comprehend the work Chyna had to do just to survive. She didn't have parents living in a penthouse on Fifth Avenue whom she could fall back on. The only safety net Chyna had was the few thousand dollars she'd managed to save over the past eight years.

"Even if you're not looking for anything serious, just have some fun for once," her friend implored. "If you're not careful you're going to burn out before you reach thirty." Holding the liquid eyeliner brush in one hand, Liani captured Chyna's chin with the other, and with a concerned plea, said, "Promise me you'll let yourself enjoy Jared."

"Depends on what you mean by 'enjoy,'" Chyna said with a guarded chuckle.

"Enjoy his *company,* not him as in *him.* At least not yet." Liani winked.

Chyna sat for a few minutes more while Liani put the finishing touches on her hair. Moments later, Liani was packed up and ready to go.

"Have fun tonight," her friend demanded. She blew Chyna an air kiss as she backed out of the door and carted her suitcase of cosmetics down the stairs.

Chyna slipped into her dress, then spent way more time than necessary trying to decide between her silver necklace or the faux pearls. She decided on the less formal, but still tasteful, silver.

She had no idea where Jared was taking her tonight, but figured simple and classy would work for ninety percent of the restaurants in New York. Twenty minutes later, Chyna walked into the Patisserie and found Jared sitting at one of the front tables.

He rose as soon as he saw her, his eyes traveling her full length.

"You look fabulous," was his greeting.

So did he. In his slacks, jacket and shirt with no tie, he'd dressed elegantly but not overly dressy.

Simple and classy. Score one for her.

"Thank you," Chyna answered. "Sorry, I'm late. Blame it on me being a girl. It always takes us longer to get ready."

"That's okay. I like girls." His mouth quirked in an infectious smile. "Are you ready to go?" he asked.

"As soon as you tell me where we're going."

"I'd rather keep it a surprise," he said, opening the door and gesturing for her to exit the bakery ahead of him.

"I'm not underdressed, am I?"

"You're perfect," he said. His simple compliment affected her way more than it should have. Just like the rest of him.

As she walked alongside Jared, Chyna once again questioned the wisdom of agreeing to this date. This was *so* not like her. At any given moment she had a dozen things to do, and having dinner with a rich football player had never made the list.

She shook off the unease and concentrated on what Liani had advised. She'd enjoy the evening for what it was, but come tomorrow, she was done. No more dipping her toes into the pool of luxury and wealth. She wasn't about to get caught up in this fairy tale.

Jared guided her half a block down to a silver Mercedes Coupe. He unlocked it and held the passenger side door open while she slid onto the cool leather. It was a nice step up from the N train.

"This car is gorgeous," she said when he sat behind the wheel.

"Thanks. I wasn't sure if you were wearing a skirt, so I didn't want to come in the SUV. Sam always hated getting into the SUV with a dress." He thumped both hands against the wheel and expelled a sigh. "And that's the last time I mention her name tonight. You have my permission to punch me if I say it again."

Chyna hesitated for only a second before saying, "I'm sorry for what she did to you, and for how publicized it all was. That had to have been hard to endure."

"It was," he said. "But no more talk about the woman whose name I will not mention. Tonight is about getting to know you, Chyna McCrea. Are you willing to let me peek inside that pretty little head of yours?"

Chyna felt her cheeks warm, but couldn't do a single thing to stop it. Her paltry attempt to remain unaffected was no match for Jared's charm.

"Just a peek," she returned. "You may get bored if there's no mystery."

"You're not boring, Chyna," he said with a seriousness she hadn't expected. "I'm guessing you just haven't had anyone to show you what it means to have fun." He leaned over the console, his mouth hovering scant inches from her ear. "Get ready, because I'm going to teach you a thing or two about how to have a good time."

Chyna inhaled a deep breath as she pulled the seat belt across her chest. "Lead the way."

Jared rolled to a stop in front of the Time Warner Building at Columbus Circle, handed his keys to the valet and came around the car. The doorman guided Chyna over to him and Jared placed his right hand at the small of her back. His fingers tingled where he touched her. This close, the soft, flowery fragrance that had suffused every inch of his car was even stronger. Jared closed his eyes for a second to soak in her scent.

When they entered Per Se, the maître d' greeted them with a broad smile. "Mr. Dawson. Welcome. Rena said you would be dining with us this evening. We have an excellent table reserved. Follow me, please."

Jared started to follow but felt a hesitation in Chyna's step. He glanced at her. "Are you okay?"

"I'm fine," she said. The overbright smile that didn't even marginally reach her eyes told a different story. She couldn't be disappointed? He'd scored a table at one of the most exclusive restaurants in Manhattan.

The maître d' led them to a table for two just to the right of the glass-fronted fireplace. It afforded a glorious view of Columbus Circle backdropped by the towering treetops of Central Park. He placed menus before each of them. "The sommelier will be with you shortly."

Seconds later, the sommelier arrived with the wine list. Jared waved off the leather-bound portfolio and said, "Give me your best suggestions."

The man rattled off several wines, with selections ranging from Napa Valley all the way to the northern region of Italy. "One of our most exclusive is a '49 Bordeaux. The Château La Conseillante is rich and vibrant and would go well with the *moulard foie gras* on tonight's menu."

Jared nodded. "Sounds good to me."

"Excuse me, but how much is a glass of that?" Chyna asked.

The sommelier's eyes snapped with surprise. He quickly recovered, answering, "It is only sold by the half bottle, madam. And that is fifteen hundred and eighty dollars."

"No way." Chyna shook her head. "I'm sorry, Jared, but absolutely not."

Caught off guard by her protest, Jared glanced awkwardly at the sommelier. "Would you give us a minute?"

"Of course." He sketched a slight bow and retreated.

Jared leaned forward, and in a hushed voice, asked, "Chyna, what's going on? You got something against red wine?"

"When a half bottle is equivalent to a month's rent, yes."

So this was a money issue? Did she think he'd ask her to split the bill at the end of the night?

Her eyes roaming the menu, she continued, "I'm not a huge fan of restaurants that don't list the prices of the food on the menu and charge a couple of thousand dollars for a bottle of wine as if it's nothing."

Jared sat back in his chair and folded his arms across his chest. "The à la carte menu is in the back. Prices are listed there."

She flipped to the back and continued her diatribe. "I get that you're a big-time football player and you're used to paying fifteen dollars for a beet salad, and—oh, for God's sake—*eighty dollars* for a steak? Seriously, eighty dollars? That's outrageous."

"It's just a steak."

"Exactly. You could get the same steak for twenty dollars at dozens of restaurants around the city. Why would you pay four times that much?"

Jared shook his head, completely baffled. Of all the things he could have imagined to put a wrinkle in their night, a debate over the cost of dinner had never entered his mind. He'd eaten at this restaurant more times than he could count. He was used to spending several hundred dollars on a meal without batting an eye; Samantha had expected no less.

He'd set out to impress Chyna by taking her to one of New York's most elite restaurants. Instead, he was in the midst of a lecture on food cost.

"You don't have to get steak," he reasoned, trying

to infuse a bit of humor into his voice. "The chicken is cheaper."

"I could buy a week's worth of groceries with that amount," she mumbled. She looked up from the menu and gave him an apologetic smile. "I'm sorry. I have a hard time controlling my practical side. This is all just so much more than I'd expected."

"We can go someplace else," he quickly said, seeing a way out of this awkward situation he'd managed to land himself in just by trying to order a bottle of wine.

She darted a quick, worried glance at the podium where the sommelier and maître d' stood. "But we're already here."

"There's no rule that says we have to stay, Chyna. And if you're going to spend the entire meal thinking about what you could have bought with each bite you swallow, I doubt you'll enjoy it. Why don't we find somewhere else?"

She bit her bottom lip and said with a tentative smile, "Really?"

For the chance to see more of those smiles, he would be willing to go Dumpster diving. Jared snatched the napkin from his lap and tossed it on the table. Chyna didn't give him a chance to reach her. She pushed her own chair back and rose. The maître d' hustled to the table.

"Mr. Dawson, is there something wrong?"

"Please apologize to Rena and thank her again for holding the table, but we won't be eating here tonight."

"I'm sorry to hear that," the maître d' said. "Is there something I can do? Suggest a less expensive wine, perhaps? We have an extensive collection."

"No, but thanks for the offer." Jared reached into his pocket and snagged a hundred-dollar bill from his money clip. He shook the maître d's hand, pressing the money into his palm.

As they waited for the valet to return with the car, Jared turned to Chyna and said, "I'm not sure where we'll find a table on such short notice on a Friday night."

"I know a few places," she said. "Do you eat Moroccan?"

Jared thought for a moment. "I don't think I've ever tried it."

"Excellent." She grinned. "I have the perfect place."

Two hours later, they were back in Brooklyn at a tiny Moroccan restaurant two blocks away from the bakery where he'd picked her up. Although the huge pillows they sat on were comfortable, Jared had lost all feeling in his left foot, but he didn't care one bit. He'd cut the damn thing off before he gave up his spot on this floor.

He scooped up a heap of couscous with a bit of pita bread and dipped it in yet another sauce. There were at least a dozen of them on their table, along with a huge bowl of couscous in the center, a platter of chicken and several bowls of vegetables that were either steamed or smothered in succulent sauces. And the twenty-dollar bottle of wine Chyna had ordered was one of the best Jared had ever tasted.

"God, this is good," Jared said around a mouthful of food.

"You should try mixing them up." She gathered a helping with her fingers and dipped it in one sauce, then another. "Here."

His heart started to jackhammer at the sight of her holding the food out for him to sample. Jared sensed the moment when she seemed to realize what she'd offered. Her eyes rounded and she began to pull her hand away, but he caught her wrist and pulled it closer. His eyes locked with hers, he closed his mouth around her fingers, dragging his teeth along her skin ever so slightly. With deliberate slowness, Jared drew each of her fingers into his mouth, licking a drop of sauce from her knuckle, swallowing the salty flavor of her skin.

"This sure beats an overpriced steak," he said.

"I'm happy you like it." The words rushed out of her mouth on a shallow breath.

Something told him he was pushing it, but Jared blocked the thought as he scooped up couscous and dipped it in several sauces. He held it out to her.

"Your turn."

Chyna hesitated a moment before leaning forward and sucking the food from his fingers.

The arousal he'd been fighting all night burst to life within his pants. Desire, potent and raw, pulsated throughout every cell in his body.

Jared squelched a groan as Chyna drew her mouth from his fingers, but he couldn't help the swift breath that escaped when she licked her lips. It took every ounce of control he possessed to stop himself from toppling the table over and capturing that delicately pink tongue.

"Thank you," she said. "That was better than I'd imagined."

It was fifteen hundred and eighty times better than he'd imagined, and that was just her mouth on his fingers. He couldn't imagine what would happen when he finally tasted that mouth with his own.

He shut his eyes for a moment, visualizing sheep in a meadow. When that didn't work to taper the erection trying to make a break for it behind his fly he tried counting back from fifty.

Chyna held up the cabernet. "Would you like more wine?"

He was seconds from bursting through his pants and she was offering wine? Forget the wine. Why wasn't she offering to swipe the food from the table and drape herself across it?

"I'm good," Jared managed to get out, though that was the understatement of the year. He was more than good. Despite their rough start at the first restaurant, tonight had been damn near perfect.

"Tell me more about the training you guys are doing at the practice facility," she said with a nonchalance that told Jared she had no idea of the state she'd put him in when she'd closed her lips around his fingers.

"Do you really want to talk about football?" he asked. "Why don't you finish telling me the story you started in the car about how you and your friend Liani first met? Sounds like that was some fight."

She rolled her eyes. "I'd hardly call it a fight. Liani didn't stand a chance. By the time we met I had been through five years of public school. She was no match for me."

"Why did she pick a fight with you?" Jared chuckled.

"Because I upstaged her at our first dance recital. She had been the best dancer at Miss Cecilia's Dance Academy until I showed up. She hated me. But all it took was one butt whipping to straighten her out."

"From what I see Liani looks pretty tough. I think you got off lucky."

"Yeah, right," Chyna huffed. She gestured to her face. "Don't let this sweet smile fool you. I can hold my own."

Lifting one hand, he lightly fingered a loose tendril of silky brown hair that rested against her cheek. "That sweet smile does all sorts of things to me. It's one of the most beautiful sights I've ever seen."

A pink hue blossomed on her creamy skin, and Jared

instantly started thinking of other ways to make her blush.

The conversation floated from her rocky start with her best friend, to which of the players kept the dirtiest locker area, to an upcoming ballet performance at Lincoln Center. Jared would rather drive rusty nails through his fingers before suffering through the ballet, but one look at the way Chyna's eyes lit up while she talked about it and he knew the first thing he'd do tomorrow was find tickets.

He didn't realize how long they'd been sitting until the attendant came to their table to tell them the restaurant would be closing in fifteen minutes. He checked his watch. It was a quarter to midnight.

"Where did the last two hours go?" Chyna asked.

"I'm not sure. I don't think either of us was too concerned with the time."

"No." She smiled. She averted her face, reaching for the small handbag she'd carried in, but Jared didn't miss the blush that had returned to her cheeks.

He braced his hands on the floor, hoping to God that his hyperaware body didn't betray him when he stood. He'd managed to calm himself down, but his control was tentative at best. One lick of her lips and he would be hard as concrete again.

He steadied himself on his feet and was able to help Chyna from the floor.

"Oh," she groaned. "I've been sitting here for way too long. I don't care how good a shape you're in, the human body isn't designed to stay in one position for an extended period of time."

Jared bit back the comment that nearly slipped out. If Samantha had made that same remark he would have countered with a suggestive reply about all the different positions the human body could get itself into.

But Chyna was not Samantha, and he had no business thinking about *positions,* or Chyna's body getting *into* those positions, or his body *joining* Chyna's in those positions.

Just stop, Jared pleaded with himself. He was two seconds away from embarrassing himself and guaranteeing there would not be a second date.

The attendant brought the bill, and Jared slipped a couple of hundreds into the leather portfolio before setting it on the table. He took Chyna by the hand, resting his palm against the small of her back.

"Okay, Jared. I eat here often enough to know that the bill didn't come even close to two hundred dollars. What did you leave…a seventy-percent tip?" she asked as they exited the restaurant and headed down the street toward the bakery where he'd met her for dinner.

Jared shrugged off her question. "We occupied one of their tables for over three hours. Consider it rent."

She huffed out a derisive laugh. "The way you ball players throw money around is just…I don't know."

Jared stopped walking and captured her elbow, halting her steps. "I don't just throw money around," he said.

"How can you say that when you were willing to pay three thousand dollars for a bottle of wine?" she asked.

"I didn't say that I don't enjoy myself. I work hard for my money, Chyna, and I don't consider splurging on a bottle of good wine wasteful. Now if I bought ten bottles of wine, brought them home and took a bath in them, *that* would be wasteful."

Her mouth twisted in a wry grin. "I heard about Lester Franklin's Perrier- Jouët bath after the Sabers won their division last year."

"He's lucky the garbage collectors didn't tell the press that he's a raging alcoholic," Jared snorted. "I respect money too much to ever do something that irresponsible, but I won't live like a pauper, either. I make a good living. Why not enjoy it?"

She remained silent, shrugging her shoulders.

Jared captured her hands and squeezed them lightly. "Is the money issue going to be a problem between us?"

Her brows hiked up. "There's an *us*? When did that happen?"

"When I sucked couscous from your fingers," he answered. She choked on a laugh. "Come on, Chyna. You know you enjoyed yourself tonight."

She pulled her hands away and continued her stroll toward the bakery. "I'll admit you were a bit of a surprise. Any man who will listen to me rant about the *Grey's Anatomy* season finale is pretty darn special."

They arrived at the narrow storefront of the Patisserie, stopping under the bakery's blue-and-yellow-striped awning. Jared trailed his fingers along her arm. "So, when do we get to do this again?" he asked.

"Let me get back to you on that," Chyna said after a pause. He was about to counter her brush-off, but she held her hand up. "I have a paper I'm working on for school, and I don't want to commit to anything until I finish the rough draft."

Jared accepted her answer with a reluctant nod. "Guess I'll have to live with that," he said. The little voice that had warned him about moving too fast reared its head again, but Jared mentally swatted it away as he shifted forward and lowered his head. "In the meantime, I think I need something to tide me over while I wait for your answer," he whispered, bending slightly and claiming her lips in a slow, gentle kiss.

The contact sent a shock of arousal spiraling through his bloodstream. Her lips were warm, tangy with the flavor of the spicy food they'd eaten at dinner. Jared brought his hand up to caress the back of her neck, tilting her head to the side and deepening the kiss.

The minute she opened her mouth and welcomed his tongue inside, the desire coursing through his veins moved swiftly to his groin, stiffening the erection that had been threatening to erupt all night. He ran his hands down her spine, settling them at the small of her back, pulling her body flush against his.

She melted against him, arching her back and sinking into his embrace. But then her hands snaked up his chest and gently, but firmly, pushed him away.

"Stop," she said, her breath coming in shallow, rapid pants.

Jared took a step back, his breathing as ragged as hers. His gaze settled on Chyna's lips, dusky rose and slightly swollen from their kiss.

"I'm sorry," she said. "I just…it was moving a little too fast."

"That's okay, Chyna. I was only expecting dinner tonight, remember?" he said with a tinge of humor to his voice.

She picked up on it, returning a shy smile. "I had a lovely time," she said. "But I think it's time for me to go."

"Let me walk you to your door," he offered, hating the thought of her leaving him, even though their date had lasted several hours longer than he'd anticipated.

"This is fine. I don't live too far from here."

"I don't like the idea of you walking home alone at this time of night," he said.

"I've been doing it for years." She laughed. "No,

really. I think the chivalrous thing is kind of sweet, but I'll be fine." She took a step forward and placed a chaste kiss on his cheek. "Thanks for a lovely evening, Jared." She gave him one last smile before pivoting and walking down the street.

Jared stood under the striped awning, staring at her retreating form until she turned and disappeared around a corner. He wasn't an expert at having meaningless flings, but Jared had a feeling he'd gotten this all wrong. What he was feeling at the moment was as far from meaningless as a person could get.

But he wasn't complaining.

Chapter 7

Chyna placed the overloaded laundry basket she'd carried up from her parents' basement next to the other two at her mother's feet.

"Do you have enough starch, or should I make a store run?" she asked her mother, who was ironing the collar of her housekeeping uniform into a fine point.

"I have a secret stash in the cabinet under the sink," her mom answered with a wink.

Chyna drew several shirts from the basket and draped them across the arm of the sofa, smoothing out whatever wrinkles she could.

"Chyna, you don't have to do that," her mother said.

With a sigh, she said, "I figure you can use whatever help you can get. You look so tired, Mom."

Selena McCrea shrugged the shoulder that was working the iron back and forth. "I worked a double shift at the hotel yesterday."

"So put this away and rest for a bit," Chyna implored. "The laundry doesn't have to be done this very minute."

"If I don't do it now, it'll only continue to pile up. I spent most of last week bringing your father from one doctor appointment to another. I didn't get any housework done around here. Thank goodness my next shift doesn't start for another few hours."

"You have to work again tonight after working a double shift yesterday?"

Her mother set the iron on its base and held out her hand. "What else am I supposed to do, Chyna? I don't have a money tree, just a fake ficus."

Fake ficus, Chyna mouthed with her. The saying had been a staple of her childhood. "I worry about you, Mom."

"I know, honey, but you don't have to. I'm used to it."

"Yeah, that's the problem," Chyna murmured. Her mother had spent so many years working double shifts that her body would probably recoil if she actually took a day off.

"I'm sorry I haven't been around to help out more, but with work and school, and this new job with the Saberrettes…" Chyna swallowed down the excuses. They all seemed trite as she took in the dark smudges under her mother's eyes. It didn't matter what she had on her plate, if she didn't make time to lend her mother a hand after the years her mother had spent working to provide for her, what good was she?

"I promise to help out more, Mom," Chyna offered.

"You have enough going on. I can handle everything around here. Even with that cranky man upstairs," she said with a tired smile.

As if to add the punctuation to her mother's statement, a stream of heavy coughing filtered down from the upstairs bedroom.

"Should I check on him?" Chyna asked.

Her mother raised a hand. There was one last cough and a loud wheeze, then nothing. She shook her head. "He's fine."

The coughing started up again, worse than before.

"Then again," her mother said, setting the iron down.

"No, Mom." Chyna put a hand to her shoulder. "I'll check him. I wanted to say hello before I leave anyway."

She walked up the narrow steps that were covered in the same threadbare paisley runner that had been there since she was a little girl. Without thought, she automatically skipped over the second to the last step to avoid the creak that had been there as long as the runner.

The door to her parents' bedroom was open, another string of coughs meeting her as she poked her head in.

"Everything okay in here?" she asked.

"China Doll? I didn't…didn't know you were…here."

She walked into the room and perched on the edge of the bed. At one time, resentment toward her father surfaced nearly every time she saw him. But how could she feel anything but pity for what he had become: a weak shell of a man who could barely walk two steps without having to rest.

But he could have been so *much more.*

If only he'd stuck with his singing. Her father had been gifted with an amazing voice, but for reasons Chyna would probably never understand, he just gave up on his goals of singing professionally. It still infuriated her to think of how much their entire family had sacrificed for his aspirations, only to have him quit before realizing his dream.

She took a deep breath, suppressing her acrimony. There was no point in rehashing these old frustrations.

"Just stopped by to see how you two were doing," Chyna said. "I'm sorry I haven't been by more often, but things have been so busy this summer."

"How is work going?" he asked, then followed the question with a fit of coughing that had his body lifting from the bed.

"I'm getting closer to that promotion," Chyna said. "I should hear something about it in the next few weeks."

"And school?"

"I'll have my degree by the end of the summer semester," Chyna said. "With honors, I might add."

"That's my China Doll," he said.

Chyna hesitated a moment, debating the wisdom of mentioning the freelancing job.

"I've got some news," she started. "I took on a second job."

A spark shone in her father's gray eyes that were so much like her own. "Working hard…like your old man used to…huh, baby girl? What's…the job?"

Chyna steeled herself against the inevitable backlash. "I'm the new choreographer for the New York Sabers cheerleading squad."

A sour look came over her father's face. "You're never going to learn, are you, China Doll?"

Chyna's hand fisted at her side. "What's wrong with working as a choreographer?"

"It's a waste…of time," her father said.

Chyna shot up from the bed. She paced along the area rug in front of the dresser. "I just don't get you. Most parents encourage their children's dreams. You've spent your entire life trying to squash mine."

"Because I know…what it's like to never see your dreams…come true."

"You never *gave* your dream the chance to come true, Dad! God." She raked a stiff hand through her hair. The resentment she'd tried to stave off returned full force. "I lost count of how many days you missed work because you heard that there was some talent scout holding auditions. Then you'd back out at the last minute. How many birthdays and Christmases passed without anyone getting presents because you'd spent the money recording demo tapes? And where are those tapes now? Stacked in the closet because you never sent them to any of the record companies you claimed were just waiting to discover you." Her voice shook with anger and disappointment. "After all the time and energy you spent on your music, you never did anything with it."

Chyna pointed to her chest. "I'm not going to make your mistakes," she said. "This position with the Saberrettes is a *paying* job. It's a huge stepping-stone."

"It's a waste of time," her father said, cutting her off. "You saw what happened…with me. How many times… do I have to tell you…to let that…silly dream go?"

"No," Chyna said softly. She looked her father in the eye, years of hurt and resentment clogging her throat. "I refuse to let it go."

Just because he'd given up on his dreams, that didn't mean she had to follow in his footsteps.

After all these years, how could he not see what his lack of ambition had cost his family? Her mother could barely keep her eyes open after working a double shift, because her husband was too sick to work at any of the meager jobs he'd held while waiting to be "discovered." Last night, Chyna had nearly ruined her date with Jared because a lifetime of having to watch every single penny had made it impossible for her to stomach eating in a fancy restaurant.

If her dad had seriously pursued his music, who knows what he could have become? Instead, he'd spent years going from one minimum wage job to another and singing for tips in neighborhood bars. He'd wasted his talent, yet he blamed everyone else for the way his life had turned out.

Chyna quelled the urge to lash out at him again. What good would it do?

With a sigh, she walked over to the bed. "I'm sorry for yelling," she said, placing a kiss on her father's forehead. "I have to get going, Dad. I'll try to drop in again soon. Take care of yourself."

"You, too…China Doll."

Chyna pulled in a deep breath, wishing things could have been different. Wishing *he* could have been different.

She could spend a lifetime wishing—in a way, she already had—and it wouldn't make a bit of difference. Her father would never change. Thank God she'd learned from his mistakes.

When she arrived back downstairs her mother's eyes were glued to the television where a panoramic view of a golden beach at sunset beckoned like a hot bath after a long day's work.

"Watching the Travel Channel again?" Chyna motioned to the television.

"That's Corfu, Greece. It's one of the ports on this ten-day Mediterranean cruise." The wistfulness in her mother's voice created an ache deep within Chyna's chest.

"You'll get there one day," Chyna said.

Her mother looked away from the television long enough to give her a tired smile.

Chyna was a long way from being able to afford to send her mother on a Mediterranean cruise, but maybe if she got the promotion she could treat her to a spa day. Her mother deserved some time off, even if it was just one day to put her feet up and just *be,* for God's sake.

"I need to get to the dance school," Chyna said, walking over to her mother and placing a kiss on her cheek. "You'll let me know if you need anything, won't you, Mom?"

"Of course," she said.

Yeah, right. Her mother could be standing in the middle of a desert and wouldn't admit to needing a glass of iced water.

Chyna grabbed her purse on her way out the door and headed for the subway, taking in the seventy-degree temperature and clear skies. Every time winter had her contemplating leaving New York for some place with sun, spring came along and reminded her of what was fabulous about this city.

She pulled out her cell phone to check the time. She still had an hour before she had to be back in Brooklyn for her first dance class. She was teaching jazz to the eight- to twelve-year-olds and later this afternoon she was leading an adult salsa lesson. She texted Valerie, another unpaid volunteer at the school, and asked her to download Gloria Estefan's "Caridad" from iTunes for today's lesson.

Before she could put her phone back into her purse, it started ringing. Chyna's heart immediately started beating faster at the number illuminated on the screen.

"Hello," she answered.

"I've been trying to eat breakfast, but I don't have anyone to hand-feed me. Your sweet fingers have ruined me."

Chyna choked on a laugh. "Unless you're eating cous-cous for breakfast, you should probably use a fork, not fingers."

"Your fingers could feed me anything," he said.

His words set off a scintillating chain reaction that tumbled to all her extremities. An acute, sensual aware-ness that had been simmering since last night's kiss rushed to the surface, heating her skin.

"Did you finish that paper you were working on?" Jared asked.

"It's not something I can finish in one night. I've been working on that paper for nearly two months."

He groaned. "Are you telling me I have to wait two months before I can eat from your fingers again?"

"There will be no eating from fingers, no matter when you see me again," Chyna stated. "Apparently, it's too much for you to handle."

"Oh, I can handle it," he said.

Sweet Lord. When his voice dipped to that deep, sexy timbre, it was all she could do not to moan.

"I really have to work, tonight, Jared. I'm nearly done. If I pull an all-nighter, I can probably complete the first draft."

"Does that mean I can see you tomorrow?"

"Didn't you just see me last night?"

"Yes, and I really liked what I saw. Makes me want to see it again, and again and again."

Her breath hitched at his admission.

"Jared," she started. "I…" But she couldn't verbalize what she wanted to say. Because she wasn't exactly sure of what *to* say.

She'd told herself their date was a one-time deal. It didn't matter that she'd laughed more last night than she had in months. Or that for nearly four hours she hadn't thought once about school or work or the rent check that was due in two days. God, it had felt *so* good to leave that stuff behind.

She could afford just one more evening of enjoying herself, couldn't she?

"What did you have in mind?" Chyna heard herself ask.

A devilish smile curved up the corners of Jared's mouth. Lounging in his media room, he flipped back to the previous defensive series on the muted television and pressed the play button.

"Since I was adventurous enough to try your Moroccan food, I thought I'd test your level of adventure," he said.

"What kind of test are we talking about here?"

His grin widened at the reluctance he heard in Chyna's voice. "Jet Skiing," he answered, bracing himself for her response.

"Absolutely not!"

Jared couldn't hold in his laugh. "Are you scared?"

"Not scared, just…smart," she replied. "I try not to intentionally put myself in a position to suffer brain damage."

"This from a woman who spent the last week practicing dance moves just steps away from three-hundred-pound guys crashing into each other?"

There was a pause before she said, "Touché. But I'm still not getting on a Jet Ski."

Jared paused the film and walked over to the bar to grab a bottled water from the wine chiller. "Who would have thought there was such a coward hiding behind those pretty gray eyes," he said.

"Don't try your reverse psychology on me. I'm not falling for it."

"Fine," he relented. "No Jet Skis. Why don't you decide?"

A few seconds went by before she asked, "How do you feel about dog parks?"

He twisted the cap from his water and took a swig. "Since I don't have a dog, I'm pretty ambivalent on the subject."

"I've been neglecting Summer, and I promised her we'd spend tomorrow afternoon at the dog park."

"And she understood your promise?"

"Of course she did."

Jared shook his head. "I just love the way pet owners like to pretend their pets have human qualities."

"Hey, Summer is smarter than half the people in New York. Now, if you want to see me tomorrow, you meet me in Madison Square Park. I'll buy you lunch."

"Only if you let me buy you dinner tomorrow night," he said. "Don't say no," Jared entreated, sensing her hesitation. "I thought we established last night that you, me and dinner make a good combination."

"It did, but—"

"No buts, Chyna." He cut off her refusal before she had the chance to voice it. "You had fun last night. Don't tell me you didn't."

"I already admitted that I did."

"And I enjoyed showing you a good time. What objection can you have to doing that again?"

"You'll eventually want to take it further, and I just don't have time to devote to anything serious," she said.

He leaned back against the bar and crossed his ankles in front of him. "I'd be lying if I said I wasn't disappointed when you ended that kiss, or that I haven't thought about it a time or two—" or two hundred, he thought "—since last night. But I've already promised not to push you any further than you're willing to go.

"I like you, Chyna." As he said the words, Jared realized he meant them. Completely. "The only thing I had to look forward to this summer was working out at the practice facility and coming back to this empty house to watch tape. The promise of seeing you, it's more than I could have hoped for."

She was quiet for several long moments before finally saying, "That was one of the sweetest things anyone has ever said to me."

"I meant it," Jared said, imagining the smile on her face and feeling like a king for knowing he'd put it there. "What time should I meet you at the park?" he asked.

"One o'clock," she answered. "How should I dress for dinner?"

A sense of triumph welled in his chest at her acquiescence. "I won't make the same mistake twice," Jared said. "We'll go casual tomorrow."

"Enjoy watching your tape," she said.

"Good luck with the paper tonight," he returned.

"Thanks," she said. "Goodbye, Jared."

"Goodbye, Chyna."

After a beat, she said, "Are you hanging up, or what?"

"You go first," Jared prompted.

"And we've both just landed back in the sixth grade," she said with a droll snort. "I'll see you tomorrow." She disconnected the call.

He'd smiled so much in the last ten minutes, his jaw ached, yet Jared still couldn't wipe the stupid grin from his face.

He went into the kitchen and pulled out the turkey on wheat Maggie had left in the fridge for him. Unwrapping the clear plastic wrap, Jared ambled over to the phone on the counter and dialed into his voice mail.

He deleted the first three calls, two from his agent and another from the building concierge. The fourth was from his mom, letting him know she'd made it to Okinawa where she was spending the month with his sister, Sharon, while his navy doctor brother-in-law served his fourth tour in Afghanistan.

He skipped to the fifth missed call. It was from his business partner, Patrick.

"We got the go-ahead," Patrick's excited voice said over splotches of cell phone static. "Inspection is Monday. I'm meeting the contractor at noon tomorrow. Come over if you have time."

Jared finished off his sandwich and headed to his bedroom to change. He'd made an attempt to help out more with the Red Zone, but he was so used to being a silent partner in the many ventures he invested in, he had never gotten around to giving Patrick a hand. If he'd been thinking clearly, Jared would have gotten more involved. Helping Patrick bring his concept of an upscale, sports-themed barbershop to life would have helped to keep his mind off Samantha these past six months.

Of course, now that he'd started whatever it was he and Chyna had going on, he didn't need anything else to occupy his mind. She had taken up all available space and then some.

Jared locked up his penthouse and hopped into his car. A half hour later, he spotted Patrick's car parked in the alley beside the two-story brownstone Jared had purchased in Upper Manhattan's Morningside Heights neighborhood. A contractor had gutted the interior and completely renovated it.

Patrick Foley greeted him just inside the entrance to

the barbershop. Jared clasped his college roommate on the shoulder. "Give me the grand tour."

"Prepare yourself, my man," Patrick said with a gigantic grin. They set out on a tour of the shop, Patrick pointing out the features that had been added since the last time Jared had visited. "The waiting area has four televisions dedicated to four main sports—football, basketball, baseball and hockey. Unless there's a major golf or tennis tournament going on."

They walked up three steps to the main area of the barbershop. Dark hardwood floors gleamed. The right side housed seven barber stations separated by clear, shoulder-high partitions. Each station was comprised of a heated leather massage chair, a stainless-steel sink, and a nineteen-inch flat-screen television extending eye-level from a long metal arm.

The left wall held a bar with a movie-theater caliber popcorn maker and three beer taps, along with two additional stations for shaving and a towel warmer the size of a refrigerator.

"I would live here," Jared said.

Patrick laughed. "Well, there's an extra bedroom upstairs. You are always welcome to it if Sam ever puts you—" His friend stopped. "Damn, man, I'm sorry."

"Don't sweat it," Jared said.

"It's just that you two were together for so long, it's easy to forget that she's gone."

For months he'd had that same problem, but Jared realized he hadn't thought much about Samantha this past week. Not since he'd looked across the practice field at the Sabers facility and encountered a vision with gray eyes and a body to die for walking toward him.

"Let me show you the rest," Patrick said. He pointed out all the features that made the Red Zone different from your normal barbershop. A guy could spend his entire Saturday here. This place was a surefire goldmine.

"How are the plans coming for the grand opening?" Jared asked.

"It's all good," Patrick said. "I've got ad spots running on four radio stations starting on Wednesday. The Facebook page launched last night. And I just confirmed with the Sabers' public relations that we'll have three cheerleaders."

"You're bringing in Saberrettes?"

"Hell, yeah," Patrick said. "I thought I told you about that. The free beer and pizza may bring guys in the door, but girls in skimpy outfits will keep them here."

Jared couldn't argue with that logic. "You need anything else?" he asked. "You know, cash-wise, to help buy streamers and balloons or whatever else it is people use to decorate for a grand opening?"

"I've got it covered," Patrick said. "You've done enough. I don't know how I'm going to repay you for this, man."

"Easy, you'll write me a nice check every month." Jared laughed.

"Yeah, I know." Patrick joined in with a chuckle. "Still, I owe you. After the divorce, not a single bank was willing to give me a loan. I needed this."

"You know you can always count on me," Jared said, bringing his long-time friend in for a one-armed hug. "Now why don't you start paying me back by ordering a pizza while we watch the Celtics and Lakers?"

"You got it." Patrick clamped a hand on his back as he fired up one of the flat screens.

Chapter 8

"Summer, no!" Chyna called in a stern voice. She bent down and scooped Summer into her arms before her tiny canine explorer could find another flower to chew. Nuzzling her Yorkie's neck, she said, "Why do you insist on eating the grass? You'll have these people thinking Mommy doesn't feed you."

Summer's pink tongue darted out and gave Chyna's nose an apologetic lick, but as soon as the dog was on all fours again she darted for the foliage. Chyna tightened her grip on the leash, shaking her head at her ill-behaved baby.

"Looks like she's trying to get away from you."

The sound of that deep, amused voice caused a delicious ripple to travel from her shoulders to the small of her back. Chyna turned and forgot what she was going to say; the sight of Jared rendered her speechless. He wore tan deck shorts and a plaid shirt of light blue, tan and white. It was unbuttoned to reveal a white tank underneath that hugged his washboard abs. Expensive sunshades covered his eyes.

Sweet Jesus, the man looked good.

"Hi," Chyna said, surprised that she had use of her tongue when it was still hanging halfway out of her mouth.

"I thought you said one o'clock," he said. "It's not even twelve-thirty."

She gestured to the dog sniffing inquisitively at Jared's dark brown sandals. "Summer was getting restless, so we came a little early."

"Restless, huh?" Jared fell to his haunches and went straight for Summer's ears, scratching the spot that automatically sent the dog's right leg to tapping. Chyna knew with that one move, Jared had become Summer's new best friend. She wondered if he could zero in on *her* spot that quickly.

"Stop it." Chyna chastised herself.

She realized she'd spoken aloud when Jared looked up at her and asked, "Why? She likes it."

"Not you. I'm sorry," she said with an offhand wave, while her stomach knotted with an anxious ache that had been there since their kiss on Friday. "So, are you hungry? I'm buying you lunch, remember?"

"Will it involve you slipping your fingers into my mouth?" he asked with a decadent grin.

Chyna's stomach instantly clenched with need, and a sudden throb starting humming between her thighs.

"They do sell some of the best French fries you'll ever taste," she answered, surprised by the huskiness in her tone.

"If they're coming from your fingers, then I have no doubt."

Oh, but this one was dangerous. The man had more sexual magnetism in his left pinky than the last three guys she'd dated combined. The fact that the last date she'd been on before Jared had been well over a year ago made the situation even more perilous. If she wasn't careful Chyna knew she would get way more than she'd bargained for when she agreed to kicking back and having a little fun. The look in Jared's eyes promised way more than just a *little* fun.

Chyna gave Summer's leash a tug and they headed toward the corner of the park at Twenty-third Street and Madison Avenue, where the Shake Shack, a popular burger stand, was located.

"How'd the paper writing go last night?" Jared asked, retrieving the sunshades he'd hooked over the collar of his shirt and placing them on his eyes.

"I stayed up way too late finishing the first draft, which is why I'll probably fall asleep in the middle of eating my hamburger."

"I remember those days." Jared laughed. "The worst was philosophy. I hated that class."

"I wouldn't think philosophy would be popular with football players," Chyna remarked.

"It wasn't, but I was a political science major. It was required."

"Political science? What did you plan to do with that?"

"Law school," he answered nonchalantly.

Chyna nearly stumbled. "Ooo-kay, I *so* wasn't expecting that."

"Not typical of your average football player?" he asked with a grin. "I know, but I come from a family of high achievers. It's what was expected of me."

"Don't tell me the multimillionaire football player is the underachiever in the family?" she scoffed.

He chuckled. "Money-wise, I'm winning the race," he said. Then he shrugged again. "My dad's a navy doctor and my younger sister married a navy doctor. They're stationed in Japan. In fact, my mom is there right now."

"What does your sister do?"

"She's working on her Ph.D. in…wait for it…philosophy."

"Ouch!" Chyna laughed. "And you couldn't even get into law school. The shame."

He ran a hand over his close-cut hair. "I actually got into a few, but I decided football would be more fun. Is that the line?" Jared pointed to the procession of people snaking around the southeast corner of the park.

"That would be it," Chyna confirmed. "This is typical of a Sunday afternoon. The Shake Shack is known for their burgers, fries and shakes."

"How come I've never heard of this place? Looks like everyone else in New York has."

"Well, their wine list isn't very extensive," she teased.

He halted his steps. "Will I ever live down that bottle of wine?"

"Not anytime soon," Chyna said with a breezy laugh.

They made their way to the back of the line, but then Chyna was immediately treated to one of the perks of being in the company of a celebrity. People began giving up their spot in line as soon as they recognized Jared. Moments later, a teen in a turquoise Shake Shack T-shirt greeted them and escorted them to one of the tables under the towering trees of Madison Square Park.

"It's so exciting to have you here." The girl beamed. "What would you like to order? It's on the house."

Chyna was stunned, yet Jared carried on as if this red carpet treatment was no big deal.

"Two burgers, two fries and two shakes," Jared said. "Are you a chocolate or vanilla person?" he asked her.

"Chocolate," she uttered. "And a bottle of water, if that's okay?"

"Absolutely," the girl answered. "I'll bring it right out."

Chyna gestured to the girl's retreating form. "What just happened there?"

Jared grinned. "Welcome to my world. Nice isn't it? I would never have gotten this type of treatment if I had gone to law school."

"Unbelievable." She shook her head. "You ball players are so spoiled."

"We're used to getting what we want." His grin was the epitome of sexy.

Gazing at his face, which was streaked with slashes of sunlight filtering between the branches high above, Chyna tilted her head to the side and asked quietly, "And just what is it you want, Jared Dawson?"

For a moment he didn't say anything, just continued to stare at her. Slowly, one side of his incredibly decadent mouth tipped up. He leaned forward and crossed his arms over the table.

"I'd tell you," he divulged in a suggestive whisper, "but it would scandalize Summer's innocent ears. Maybe I can show you later, once we've tired her out."

His bold proposal settled erotic and hot in Chyna's belly. She was saved from responding with the arrival of their food. For the next ten minutes Chyna watched in awe as Jared polished off his burger, his fries and half of hers, along with the super thick milkshake.

He leaned back in the rickety chair and patted his stomach, which was still tight as a drumhead. How incredibly unfair was that?

"Now I understand why people wait in line for an hour." He reached down and picked up Summer from where she'd been resting at Chyna's feet. "Okay, Summer, what do you say we work off some of this food?"

Summer yelped, her tail wagging excitedly. The little traitor. A bit of attention from a cute boy and the dog forgot all about her mommy. Looking at said boy as he rose from the table, Chyna couldn't blame Summer one bit.

"Do we have doggy toys?" Jared asked over his shoulder.

"We never leave home without them," Chyna answered.

They walked over to a patch of grass toward the center of the park. She usually didn't detach Summer from her leash, but Chyna figured with both of them there, one of them would be able to track the dog down if she took off. She unclipped the leash, handed Jared the dumbbell-shaped chew toy from her backpack and parked herself on a patch of even ground under a shade tree.

For the next twenty minutes, Chyna laughed until her side hurt as Summer ran Jared in circles. She was quick as a whip, catching the dumbbell and racing it back to Jared before he had the chance to catch his breath. Sometimes Summer would run up to Chyna and waggle her toy just out of Chyna's reach, then take off again for Jared.

A chime started from within the backpack. She reached in for her cell phone. It was Liani.

"Hey there! What's going on?" Chyna answered.

"Hey, yourself. Did you get your paper done last night?"

"Finally finished the first draft," Chyna said.

"Good. Now you won't have any reason to cancel our girl's night out again."

Chyna's eyes followed Jared's strong, lean body as he chased Summer. Despite the casual attire, there was no mistaking the powerfully built male underneath those clothes. She didn't want to burst Liani's bubble, but Chyna had a feeling the cancellations would continue.

"Yeah," was all she managed to say.

"Good, I'll plan something fun," Liani answered. "Oh, before I forget, a couple of girls from the squad have a promotional event on Saturday. There's some hotshot barbershop opening in Morningside Heights, not too far from Columbia University, and they want the Saberrettes for the grand opening. I think you should come. You can see another side of what we do."

"I'll need to check my schedule, but if I can make it, I'm there," Chyna said.

"Meet me at my folks' place. We can go together," Liana said.

"You'll still be at your parents?"

"Yes." Liani sighed. "When the maintenance guy went in to fix my shower, he discovered a whole mess of problems with the piping. I won't be able to move back into my apartment for at least another two weeks."

"Poor you. Stuck in a fancy penthouse on Fifth Avenue for another two weeks," Chyna drawled.

"Want to trade places?" Liani asked.

"No thanks." Chyna laughed at her friend's colorless tone. "Email me the specifics about the event. I'll talk to you later, okay?"

"Sure. And, hey," Liani said before Chyna could hang up. "You still owe me the dirt on your date with Jared Dawson. Don't think I forgot."

"I know," Chyna said. Jared scooped up Summer and started walking toward her. Chyna bit her lower lip. "He's coming this way. I'll tell you about it later."

"Wait! You're with him now! Chy—"

Chyna ended the call and tossed the phone next to her hip. Using one hand to shield her eyes from the sun, she looked up at him and smiled. "Worn out yet?"

Jared parked himself next to her and Summer scampered onto his lap and immediately started to lick his face. "This dog would give the Energizer Bunny a run for its money," Jared huffed on an exhausted breath.

Chyna reached over and pulled Summer from his chest. "Come here, you. You are such a traitor. It's not nice to ignore Mommy."

"How's Mommy doing?" Jared asked, leaning back on an elbow. His sexy grin started all manner of yummy things swirling in the pit of Chyna's stomach. His teeth were perfect, straight and gleaming white. She'd never noticed the dimple indenting his cheek. Add that to the list of unfair advantages that had been heaped onto Jared Dawson. There had to be something wrong with him. Anyone lucky enough to have dimples should at least have to suffer from some type of fungus or skin disorder. It was the way the world maintained balance.

"Didn't know something this small could have so much energy, did you?" Chyna laughed.

"What's even more amazing is that she never gets bored. You would think running after that stupid dumbbell would get old after a while."

"Not for her." Chyna shook her head. "She could go on for hours."

"Speaking from experience?" She could hear the laughter in his voice.

She returned his grin as she placed Summer on the grass. Summer immediately found a stick twice her size and pounced on it, wiggling her head back and forth and growling.

"She's bloodthirsty," Jared said.

"Yeah, that stick doesn't stand a chance." Chyna turned back to him, unable to wipe the smile from her face. "Do you have a pet?"

"Nah. Tried to keep a plant a few years ago, but managed to kill it within a month."

She rolled her eyes. "That is pitiful."

"It's hard to keep up when we have back-to-back away games. We're either on airplanes, in hotels or at the Sabers compound. My housekeeper brought in a few plants, but I still don't know if they're real or fake. She takes care of them. But I couldn't ask her to do that for a dog. Besides, Sam wasn't an animal person."

He glanced at her then back out over the park. "I'm bracing myself," he said.

"For what?" Chyna asked.

"You're supposed to punch me for mentioning her name."

Instead of punching him, she scooted over and nudged his shoulder with her own. "I'm not going to punch you. It's unrealistic to think that you can just wipe her out of your mind." Chyna picked up a blade of grass and trailed it under her nose. "How long were you two together?"

"Ten years," he answered after a pause.

She winced. "That's even longer than I thought." She hesitated a moment before asking, "Do you want to talk about it?"

"Not a chance," Jared answered. "No more talk about old girlfriends, or my overachieving family or anything else about me," he said. "I want to talk about you."

"What do you want to know?"

"Why don't we start with what you do when you're not teaching cheerleaders new dance moves or burying your face in schoolbooks? I know you work for a hedge fund, but what do you do?"

"Risk assessment," she answered. Actually, she did administrative tasks for the people who did risk assessment, but why share those details?

"Sounds, uh, fun I guess?" he said wearily.

"I'll admit it's not the most entertaining job." Chyna laughed. "But I've done okay for myself. I'm up for a promotion. Besides, that job isn't supposed to be fun. I have dance for that."

"You really love dancing, don't you?"

She looked over at him and smiled. "I really do." Chyna shook her head and said with a wistful sigh. "This new job with the Saberrettes has been like a dream."

"So why not make it a full-time gig?"

She gave him a sardonic look. "Because I have bills to pay," she said. "I think the only dancers making real money are the professional partners on *Dancing with the Stars*."

"You do that type of dancing?"

"I do all types of dancing, and yes, ballroom is one of them. I taught a salsa class yesterday at the dance school where I volunteer."

"That right? Hmm, I may have to sign up for a few private lessons," he said.

Chyna burst out laughing.

"What?" he asked with an affronted tone. "NFL players have done pretty well on *Dancing with the Stars*. Emmitt Smith won the whole thing the year he was on there."

"You're looking to join *Dancing with the Stars*?"

"It's not out of the realm of possibility," he said. "I'm pretty light on my feet."

"Well, I've seen you move across the football field, so I have to agree with you on that one."

"You've been checking me out on the field?" he asked, a bit of sexiness returning to his voice.

"Maybe," she answered, nudging him with her shoulder. The contact sent sparks of electricity shooting down her arms all the way to the tips of her fingers.

She was about to ask him how he liked playing for the Sabers when a screech just to the right of them halted her. A woman screamed, "Roscoe, no!"

Chyna looked over and saw Summer rolling on the ground with a dog twice her size. The dog snapped at her, and Summer quickly scuttled away, dashing straight into a patch of bushes with razor-sharp thorns.

Jared catapulted himself from his perch on the grass and raced over to the shrubbery where Chyna's dog was hanging by the scruff of her neck, a thick branch hooked underneath her collar. He crouched down and slipped his hand under Summer's belly, then unbuckled the collar from around her neck.

He gently extracted the dog from the thorny underbrush, making sure she hadn't been skewered by any of the three-inch thorns. It didn't look as if she'd been stabbed, just pricked. He could feel the slick blood against his fingers.

The dog shivered in his arms, whimpering as she snuggled against his chest.

"Give her to me," Chyna screamed, reaching for Summer.

Jared gently handed her the dog. "She's going to be okay," he assured her.

"I'm so, so sorry," the woman was saying. "He never goes after other dogs. I don't know what got into him."

Chyna's eyes zeroed in on Jared's chest. "Oh, my God," she screeched.

Jared looked down and noticed two splotches of blood on his white undershirt.

"She's hurt. Oh, God. Jared, she's hurt."

The dog had no more than a scratch or two; he'd checked her for injuries himself, but one look at the wide-eyed worry on Chyna's face and Jared knew what he had to do. He slipped his fingers through the crook of her arm. "Come on, there has to be a twenty-four-hour animal hospital open somewhere around the city."

He felt her shudder and realized Chyna was shaking nearly as much as the tiny dog. He stopped and wrapped his arms around them both, giving Chyna a patient, gentle squeeze. "She's going to be okay, Chyna."

There was a loud sniff, followed by a nod. "Okay," she said. "Let's just get her to the vet."

Jared jogged a couple of yards back to where they were sitting and scooped up Chyna's backpack. He took out his iPhone and searched for a twenty-four-hour animal hospital. The closest one was less than six blocks away.

"There's one on Seventeeth and Madison. It shouldn't take us too long to get there."

At his car, he held the passenger door open for her, but Chyna hesitated.

"Are you sure you're okay with this? What if she bleeds on the seat?" she asked.

Jared swallowed a curse. "It's just a car, Chyna. It can be cleaned."

They didn't talk on the short drive to the vet hospital. Chyna was too busy whispering tearful pleas for forgiveness into Summer's fur. Jared didn't like how listless the little dog looked, but he had a feeling it was more from shock than anything else. If he'd had three-inch thorns jabbing at his body, he'd be pretty shaken up, too.

He pulled in front of the brick veterinary clinic. "Bring her in. I'll be there in a minute."

He parked at a garage a few yards away from the building and rushed back to Chyna. She was sitting in a standard-issue waiting-room chair, filling out paperwork attached to a clipboard.

"Have they already taken Summer?" Jared asked.

She looked up at him and nodded. A sharp pain pierced his chest at the sight of Chyna's luminous eyes brimming with unshed tears. Jared sat in the chair next to her and wrapped an arm around her shoulders. Her hands were shaking so badly she was having a hard time filling out the forms.

"Do you want me to do this for you?" he asked.

"I've got it," she said in a small voice. She wiped at her eyes with the back of her hand and that ache in his chest sharpened.

Jared took the clipboard from her and placed it on the coffee table next to a covered glass jar filled with dog treats. He captured Chyna's shoulders in his hands and twisted her to him. He was about to reassure her again, but before he could speak she fell onto his chest, quiet sobs rising from her.

Jared ran his palm up and down her back, trying like hell to ignore how good her breasts felt pillowed against his chest. Only the lowest form of scum would use this as an opportunity to get close to her, but how could he not? She was right there, soft and vulnerable and looking to him for comfort.

He closed his eyes, relishing the moment. It felt so good to be needed again, to have a woman to take care of. Even if the only things he could provide were a few words and a comfortable place for her to lay her head.

"Ms. McCrea?" called a woman wearing scrubs dotted with cartoon dogs, cats and birds, and carrying a clipboard.

Chyna disengaged from his hold and rushed to the woman. Jared followed.

"The doctor is in with Summer now. I'll take you to—" The nurse stopped and her eyes grew huge. "Oh, my God! You're Jared Dawson!"

"Yes, I am," Jared said. "About Summer?"

"Oh, of course." She looked down at her clipboard then back up at him. "It's just that my boyfriend *loves* you. You're his favorite Saber. He has your jersey and everything."

"Helloooo." Chyna's voice approached full yell. "What about my dog?"

"Oh, right. I'm so sorry," the nurse stumbled. "Dr. Rosen is with her. I'm going to put you in one of our exam rooms. The doctor will be in soon to speak with you regarding Summer's condition."

Chyna pulled in a shaky breath and Jared ran a soothing palm down the middle of her back. "You want company?" he asked.

"Yes, please." She nodded.

They were led down a narrow, paneled corridor, into a small room with an exam table in the center and a single chair tucked into a corner. Side by side on a shelf were neatly arranged glass jars filled with cotton swabs, tongue depressors and a few other things Jared didn't recognize. Framed posters of the skeletal and muscular structure of canines and felines hung on the walls.

He tried to shake off the unease that had crept up his spine as soon as the antiseptic smell hit his nostrils.

Professional athletes and hospitals did not mix well, even when the hospitals were for species of the four-legged variety.

Jared gestured to the chair. "You want to sit?"

Chyna shook her head. "I'm too nervous. Did you see the size of those thorns? One could have taken her eye out. I know better than to let her run around without a leash. She's so nosy. She's always getting into things that she…that she shouldn't," she finished on a sob.

Jared reached for her again and brought her in for a hug. The door opened and a dark-haired woman with wire-rimmed glasses and a white coat entered. She held out her hand. "I'm Dr. Rosen," she said.

"How's Summer?" Chyna asked, wiggling out of his grasp.

"She's going to be fine. She's just a little shaken up."

"But what about the blood?" Chyna asked.

"She got nicked just below her breastbone. The technician shaved a little of her coat so I could get a better look at it, and I was able to confirm that the scratch was superficial. We'll apply an antiseptic cream and a bandage, but that's all she'll need," the doctor said with an indulgent smile. "The tech is finishing up. She should be done with her in another ten minutes. Summer is up-to-date on all her shots, correct?"

Chyna nodded.

"Good. She may be a little timid after the scare she's had. Give her some extra attention tonight."

As soon as the doctor closed the door behind her, Chyna turned and fell into Jared's arms. "I was so scared."

"Shh," he whispered into the hair just above her ear. He resumed his gentle caress up and down her back, his fingers tingling from the warmth. "I told you everything would be okay, didn't I?"

"Yes, you did," Chyna murmured against his chest. She lifted her head and stared into his eyes. "Thank you."

The words were so soft Jared barely heard them. Or maybe her voice just seemed hushed because he could hardly hear anything past the blood pounding in his ears.

Gazing at him with those brilliant gray eyes that would put Bambi to shame, Chyna slipped her hand up his neck, her fingertips applying gentle pressure at the base of his head. She tilted her face up, and it was all the invitation he needed. Jared lowered his mouth and connected with hers.

The supple give of her soft lips sent a jolt of desire shooting through his body. He glided his hand up her spine, to the back of her head, holding her in place while he melded his lips to hers. He couldn't take a second more of this closed-mouth business. Prying her lips open with his tongue, Jared plunged inside.

Good God, she tasted like heaven.

He swallowed Chyna's low moan and pulled her tighter, needing to feel her against him. It was no use denying the arousal hardening just beyond his zipper. If she didn't see how much he wanted her, she damn sure could feel it.

Still holding her to his mouth with his right hand, he snaked the other past the curve of her waist and onto her backside, cupping the firm orb in his palm and pulling her more firmly to him. His tongue darted in and out of her mouth, jousting with her tongue in a playful, erotic dance.

A hungry groan escaped her throat and she tilted her pelvis toward him.

Pleasure ricocheted against the walls of his chest.

Jared plundered her with hurried kisses, stroking the inside of her warm mouth, devouring her sweet flavor. Need quickened his blood, pulsing strong and fierce in his groin as her soft curves molded to the contours of his hard body.

The door opened and they both jumped back like two teenagers caught necking behind the bleachers.

Chyna forgot all about him as she raced to the veterinary technician and tore Summer from the woman's arms.

"Oh, baby," Chyna crooned, stroking Summer's fur and peppering her with tiny kisses.

The tech's gaze darted from Jared to Chyna. Her sly grin pretty much guaranteed that news of his kissing Chyna would be all over Facebook and Twitter before they left the vet office.

"You can take care of the bill at the receptionist's window," the tech said.

"Thank you," Chyna answered without looking up. She had eyes for only Summer.

They left the exam room and walked back to the lobby, which had gained several new occupants since they'd been gone. Jared was approached by two men, one with a handsome boxer puppy—the only breed Jared would consider if he ever got himself a dog—and the other with a hamster in a small cage. Jared signed a couple of autographs and gave the boxer a scratch behind his ears, then he went up to the counter and stood behind Chyna.

"Did she have X-rays or something?" Chyna was asking.

"No, ma'am, the doctor didn't think her injuries warranted X-rays."

"So why is the bill so much?"

"There's a two-hundred-dollar surcharge for exams

on Sundays," the woman said. "It's all itemized on your receipt."

Jared looked over her shoulder at the bill. Six hundred and forty-two dollars.

He could feel the unease rolling off Chyna. He reached into his back pocket and retrieved his wallet, pulled out his credit card and slid it on the counter. "I've got it," he told the receptionist.

Chyna slapped her hand onto the counter, covering the credit card. "No, you don't," she said.

Jared cast a quick glance at the receptionist, who was watching the two of them intently, one penciled-in brow cocked.

"Let me take care of this for you, Chyna. You weren't expecting a six-hundred-dollar vet bill when you woke up this morning."

"Six-forty-two," the receptionist said.

"I said no." Still balancing Summer in her arms, she reached into her backpack and pulled out a wallet. She passed the receptionist a credit card. A minute later, the receptionist handed it back to her.

"I'm sorry, but it was declined."

Chyna's eyelids slid shut. "Crap." She pulled out another credit card, but snatched it back before the receptionist could take it. "Wait, not this one."

Jared had to stop himself from pushing her to the side and paying the damn bill himself. He stood just behind her, looking on as her hand shook slightly while she wrote out a check.

The receptionist took the check, eyeing it cautiously.

"It's good," Chyna bit out.

The receptionist processed the check and in a few minutes they were on their way out of the animal hospital.

"I'm parked at the garage next door," Jared said quietly.

She tightened her hold on Summer and continued her march along the sidewalk. They waited in silence as the garage attendant brought his Benz around. As he pulled out onto the street, he glanced over at Chyna. "I'm not sure if I should apologize, or what," Jared said.

"No apology necessary."

"Are you sure? Because this awkward not talking thing isn't really working for me. If all it would take is an apology to make it go away, I'm willing to try it."

"I'm not comfortable with you paying for things for me," she finally said after a long pause. "I've heard stories from Liani about the unspoken rule—or maybe expectation is a better word for it—when players and girls from the Saberrettes squad hook up. But that's not me, Jared. I'm not going to put out for a nice dinner or a piece of jewelry or because you paid my dog's vet bill."

"Hey, I wasn't trying to buy my way into your pants. I was just trying to help, Chyna. Honestly," he said at the skeptical look she slid his way. "It's like I said back there, I know this was an unexpected bill. I sorta feel responsible. If I hadn't been there to distract you, you could have kept a better eye on Summer and stopped her before she ran into those bushes."

"It wasn't your fault," she murmured then turned and peered out the window.

The uncomfortable tension was like another occupant in the car. Before he could attempt another apology, Chyna said, "Can we call it a day? I'm a complete wreck and I'm tired and I just want to go home and cuddle with Summer."

"No," Jared protested, his stomach knotting at the

threat of their day coming to such a swift end. "I still owe you dinner in return for you buying me lunch."

"I didn't pay for lunch. It was on the house, remember?"

"That's beside the point," Jared said.

"I can't leave Summer alone while I go out to dinner, Jared. Not after the scare she's had."

They stopped at a red light. Jared twisted toward her. "Why don't the two of you come over to my place? I can cook…wait." He didn't know if he even had food to cook. "We can order in. Maybe watch a movie. I don't live too far from here."

"Jared," she hedged, running her hand along Summer's coat. "Look, I know that kiss back there was… um…awesome," she said after a pause. "But I don't want you getting the wrong idea. I'm not sleeping with you tonight."

He clenched the wheel and blew out a terse breath. "Chyna, that's not what this is about," he said, even though a part of him silently cursed up a storm at her pronouncement. He knew the chances of them sleeping together tonight were remote, but her baldly stated refusal cut him to the quick.

This wasn't about sex, Jared reminded himself. Besides, it would be wrong to make a move on her with her emotions still running high after Summer's accident. Sex could wait. More than anything, he wanted to put the smile she wore earlier back on her face.

"I promise to sit on the opposite end of the sofa—on the opposite side of the room, if that'll make you feel safer. I just don't want to cut our date short, Chyna."

The light changed to green, but Jared didn't move,

even when several cars behind him honked. He just continued staring at her.

"Okay," she finally relented. "But no Moroccan food. That'll just lead to trouble."

Chapter 9

An hour after stepping foot into Jared's spacious apartment, Chyna still found her mouth gaping as she discovered yet another bit of luxury. The fifteen-foot ceilings with twelve-inch crown molding were enough for her to envy him for the rest of his life. As her eyes roamed the stylish kitchen, she couldn't help but covet the state-of-the-art appliances and abundant counter space.

"I'm not sure how you can stand to leave this place," she said before biting into a slice of pizza.

He glanced around the room and grunted with an off-handed shrug. Chyna wasn't sure whether to be angry at him or feel sorry for him. His hall bathroom was nearly the size of her entire bedroom, yet it hardly fazed him. It was a shame he couldn't appreciate what he had here.

"I've been considering moving out of the city," Jared said. "If the new stadium is approved, I may look for something closer to it. Maybe Paramus."

"Some nice houses in that zip code," Chyna said.

"A bunch of the guys on the team live out that way. It's quiet, a little more private. I don't know, though. What's the point of playing for a New York team if you're not going to get the most out of the city?"

They finished off the pizza and headed to his media room. Chyna shouldn't have been shocked by the huge screen and eight captain chairs, but what girl from Queens wouldn't be taken aback by this luxury? She sat in one of the theater chairs and nearly purred as the smooth leather surrounded her. Jared placed Summer on the floor next to her. Her baby was resting comfortably on a pillow Jared had brought in from his bedroom.

He walked to an ornately carved oak cabinet and opened the door. Its shelves were lined with hundreds, possibly as many as a thousand DVDs.

"Are you in the mood to laugh, cry or scream?" Jared asked.

"What about sigh?"

"What kind of movie would that be?"

"You know, something like *Terms of Endearment* or *The Thornbirds.*" Chyna laughed at the look he tossed over his shoulder. "I'm kidding."

They settled on heart-pumping action with *The Replacement Killers,* but Chyna felt her eyes growing heavy before the first big shoot 'em up scene. When she opened her eyes again, Jared's face was inches from her own. She jerked back.

"Sorry, you just looked so damn cute," he said, scratching behind Summer's ear.

"How long have you been sitting there staring at me?"

"Since the movie ended about five minutes ago."

Chyna stifled a yawn. "I'm sorry for falling asleep. Too much excitement today, I guess."

"For both of you. This little one just woke up a few minutes ago herself."

Chyna smiled sleepily at Summer, who looked perfectly content snuggled up to Jared. Her dog was having a better date than she was. First she snuggled up to Jared's pillow, and now his chest.

She didn't want a spot on either of those surfaces, Chyna reminded herself. This was already moving way too fast. She had told herself she would have one dinner with Jared and that was it. Already they'd had two dinners and a lunch. And now look at her—curled up in his apartment with her shoes kicked off.

What had gotten into her? She hardly knew this man, yet she'd fallen asleep in his home, with only a banged-up Yorkie for protection? She never allowed herself to become this vulnerable—would never have survived this long if she had. The fact that she'd so easily let her guard down with Jared was both telling and disturbing.

"I have to go," Chyna said with an abrupt start. She searched for the release handle that would bring the reclining chair to an upright position.

"Already? It's just a little after seven," Jared said.

"I have…I like to get my clothes pressed and ready for work the night before so I'm not scrambling in the morning, you know?" She looked at him wearily. "No, you don't know." It was a stark reminder of how different their lives were.

Chyna reached over and scooped Summer out of his arms. Her body mourned the lost of the soft leather as she rose from the chair and looked around for her shoes.

"I put them over by the door," Jared said. "I didn't want you tripping over your shoes if you happened to wake up while it was still dark in here."

"Thank you." She walked over to the door and slid

her feet into her canvas slip-ons. Then she exited the media room with Jared following a few steps behind. She needed to get out of his house as quickly as possible. She couldn't think straight when she was in such close proximity to him.

"You sure you don't want to stay a little while longer for a drink or maybe a bite to eat?" Jared asked. "You didn't eat much of the pizza. I can heat up a couple of slices."

"No, thanks," Chyna said. "Really, I need to go. Now."

"Chyna." He caught her arm and turned her to him. The heated look simmering in his eyes warmed her skin.

"Jared...we shouldn't," she said, but he didn't give her a chance to voice her feeble protest. Sliding his hand up her back, to her nape, Jared captured her lips in a kiss that shot a bolt of need straight through her. His tongue nudged at the crease of her lips before plunging inside her mouth.

Chyna flattened her palms against his chest, molding her fingers to its muscled contours. A strangled moan escaped her throat as she felt his heartbeat escalate beneath her fingers. Flagrant in his sensual assault, he stroked the inside of her mouth with bold, unhurried thrusts. In and out, his tongue tempted her, coaxing her to fully engage in the erotic kiss.

Chyna melted, desire pooling between her thighs. She matched his tongue's caress stroke for stroke, drowning in the onslaught of desire that engulfed her entire being.

Jared pulled her body flush against his and the unmistakable hardness pressing against her belly knocked Chyna out of the carnal web that had ensnared her. This was moving too fast. She couldn't allow his alluring kisses to overcome her common sense.

"No," Chyna moaned. "Stop." She put her hands against his chest and managed to push him away.

Jared took a step back, his chest heaving from the lack of oxygen. "Chyna, what's wrong? You look…I don't know, scared or something. You know you never have to be afraid of me, don't you?"

But she *was* afraid. She was terrified at how quickly she'd allowed herself to become comfortable with him, with all this luxury surrounding her. This kind of life wasn't in the cards for her, and she had always been totally fine with that. She'd accepted her lot in life a long time ago, and had never wanted anything more than what she could provide for herself. Yet look how quickly she'd fallen for it after one little taste.

Jared cupped her shoulders in his large palms, his brow furrowed with concern. "Chyna, you know I would never hurt you, right?"

Maybe not physically, but he was a threat to everything she believed about herself. She didn't need Jared Dawson and his multimillion-dollar condominium. She didn't need him offering to pay her dog's vet bill, or buying her three-thousand-dollar bottles of wine.

She took care of herself. Always.

The minute she started relying on someone else to provide for her she became vulnerable. Anything could happen. Jared could get traded to another team and leave her high and dry. His girlfriend could come back, and Chyna would be left in the dust. Left to fend for herself, just as she'd been forced to do her entire life.

"I'm tired and I have a lot to do. Really, I just have to go." She picked up her backpack from the couch and headed for the door. "Thank you for today."

Displeasure shadowed his face, but he only sighed and grabbed his car keys.

Chyna shook her head. "You don't have to drive me home, Jared. I can catch the subway."

"With a dog?"

"She goes in my backpack."

"You're not catching the subway."

"Why not? I do it every other day." She held her hand up, halting his rebuttal. "I'm a big girl, Jared. I can get home on my own."

The look on his face told Chyna she'd just stepped into a battle she was going to lose. Damn him for being as stubborn as she was.

He stood before the door like an armed sentry. "You either let me drive you home, or we stay right here all night. Take your pick."

One part of her wanted to throttle him while another melted at his insistence on being a gentleman. Chyna had a feeling he'd stand there for hours before he let her go home on her own.

"Fine," she relented. "If you want to drive *all* the way to Brooklyn and *all* the way back, who am I to stop you?"

The corner of his mouth quirked up in a satisfied smile and Chyna cursed herself for giving in so easily. Jared was obviously used to getting his way.

They drove across lower Manhattan, with only the mellow R & B music that flowed from the car's surround sound speakers to break the silence. As he drove onto the Manhattan Bridge, Jared reached over and lowered the radio.

"You want to tell me why you started to freak back there?" he asked.

Chyna debated ignoring his question, but her aversion to behaving like a seventh-grader demanded she face his query head-on.

"It was moving too fast," she said, looking out at the

lights of downtown Manhattan and the Brooklyn Bridge. She turned to Jared and continued. "I don't normally do this, go up to a man's apartment after only one date."

"Technically, it was two dates," he interjected.

"We were still in the midst of date number two," she reminded him. "And that's still fast for me, Jared. I had a good time today, but I can't allow myself to be pulled in by you and all your...stuff," she said, for lack of a better word.

"My *stuff?*" he asked as he took the first exit from the bridge.

"All of this." She gestured to the opulence surrounding her. "The fancy car, the fancy condo. Even that gourmet pizza we had for dinner." Chyna shook her head. "Liani has told me countless stories about how girls from the Saberrettes squad have been sucked in by all of this. I won't let it happen to me. I'm happy with my life the way it is," she said with halfhearted conviction. "I do just fine taking care of myself."

"Okay," he said after several long, quiet moments. "So, I'll go out and buy a used Hyundai for our next date, which will be at McDonalds, by the way."

Chyna burst out laughing. Why did he have to be sweet *and* funny? And so very, very hot.

"You're obviously prejudiced against people with money," he continued. "But I can live with that."

"I am not prejudiced," she said with an affronted gasp. "I just..."

"Yes?" Jared asked when she didn't continue.

"Nothing," Chyna said.

So, maybe she did have a slight prejudice when it came to the wealthy. The thought left a bad taste in her mouth, but after struggling her entire life, it was hard not to be envious. Yet she knew money didn't bring happiness.

Just look at Liani. Despite growing up surrounded by luxury, there was a constant sadness hiding beneath the surface of Liani's quick smile and witty comebacks.

Still, there had to be an advantage to not having to worry about coming up with rent money every month. But the money thing was *her* issue. It was unfair to jump all over Jared because of her hang-ups.

"You don't have to go out and buy a used Hyundai," Chyna said. "I'll suffer the shame of riding around in your Benz."

He flashed her a grin. Cocking a brow her way, he asked, "Do you promise not to bring up money on our next date?"

"You say that as if a next date is a foregone conclusion."

"Isn't it? I was hoping Saturday night," he said. "I hate to wait that long, but I'm going to be tied up all this week with rookie tryouts."

"I thought the minicamp wasn't for another month?"

"It's not minicamp. It's tryouts. Two weeks before the NFL draft the team brings in the rookies they're interested in. We put them through all kinds of drills. See who's most ready—physically and mentally—to play on this stage."

"A job interview for football players," she commented.

"The most important interview of their careers." He turned onto her street. "Where's your place? I'm not dropping you off at that bakery again."

Chyna pointed to her building. "Just let me out here," Chyna said after noticing there wasn't an available parking spot in front of the building.

He slanted an irritated glance her way as he made an illegal U-turn and pulled into a slot on the other side of the street.

"You haven't caught on yet, have you? Didn't I tell you my father is navy? He may be a cheating SOB, but he taught his son how to be a gentleman," he said as he exited the car.

Chyna put her backpack over her shoulder and went to open the car door, but Jared had already made it to her side and was opening it for her.

Something told her to just leave it alone, but she couldn't stop herself from asking, "Your father cheated?"

Jared's forehead creased in a frown. "What?"

"You just called him a cheating SOB."

He grimaced, expelling a tired, humorless laugh. "Sorry about that," he said. "I didn't mean to be crass."

They walked up the stairs to her building's front door.

"Don't apologize," she said. "It must have been upsetting for you." Her dad may have been a bitter hard-ass, but as far as Chyna knew, he had always been faithful to her mother.

"What was upsetting was having to take care of my mom after he'd leave her to spend the night with one of his women."

Her heart broke for the suffering she heard in his voice. She reached over and squeezed his arm. "It's rough isn't it? First your dad, then your girlfriend."

Jared's lips twisted in a grimace. "Okay, we are not ending our date talking about my dad or my ex-girlfriend. That's just all kinds of wrong."

"Sorry," Chyna said, chagrined. "It does leave a bad taste in my mouth."

His brows lifted knowingly. "Only one way to get rid of that," he said, lowering his head.

Stop him, a quick stab of conscience demanded, but Chyna swatted it aside and tilted her head up. The moment Jared's soft, pliant lips touched hers, a jolt of sinfully sweet desire shot from the tips of her toes to the top of her head, leaving a tingle of want humming throughout her body. He angled his head and, with gentle insistence, pushed his tongue into her mouth.

A moan caught in the back of her throat, then escaped, sounding like a plea to her ears.

Jared must have heard it, too, because he answered with more of that tender, pleasurable pressure, dipping his tongue inside her mouth, pulling her body into direct contact with his. The touch of his powerful thighs pressed against hers ignited her insides, causing her stomach to clench with need. He clamped her backside with his hands and pulled her firmly against him. Chyna's entire body shivered with awareness as she felt his arousal pulsing against her pelvis.

Summer let out a tiny bark, and Chyna pulled back.

"Oh, baby," she exhaled on a breathy sigh, pressing a kiss to the dog's head. "Mommy's sorry." Chyna chanced a look at Jared and his hot stare nearly singed her. His chest rose and fell with his deep, labored breaths.

"I should probably go," he said with effort.

"You probably should," Chyna agreed.

Why neither of them moved was the question of the hour, but she was still too dazed to come up with a plausible answer. Instead of taking a step back, Jared took a step forward. He cupped her face in his hands and lowered his head.

But instead of another breath-robbing, toe-tingling, heart-stopping kiss, he simply brushed his lips on her forehead before letting her go. He walked down the building's steps and stood on the sidewalk.

"It might be dangerous for me to walk you to your apartment's front door, but I'm going to stand here until you call and tell me you're safely inside."

"You don't have to do that," Chyna said.

"Why are you arguing with me, woman?"

Chyna couldn't help her grin. She unlocked the door to the building, then quickly made it up the stairs and into her apartment. Stooping to put down Summer—who immediately ran to her water bowl—Chyna closed the front door and leaned against it. She pulled her phone out of her backpack and called Jared.

"I made it safely up the stairs. You can leave now."

"How do I know you're safe? How do I know there wasn't some masked gunman waiting for you, and he's not just making you say that so I can leave?"

Chyna walked over to the window and pulled up the shade. She unlocked it and pushed the window open. "No gunman," she called.

Jared looked up from where he stood just below her window, the phone still to his ear. "I'm starting to think I should come up there to make sure," he spoke into the phone, his voice low and seductive.

"I think that's a bad idea," Chyna returned. Because it sounded like a really, *really* good idea.

"I'm going to teach you how to have fun one of these days," Jared said.

"The Shake Shack, a visit to the animal hospital and ten minutes of an action film, and you say I don't know how to have fun? What more do you want?" she asked.

"Let me come up there and I'll show you."

Oh, he was bad. The good kind of bad. The *really* good kind of bad.

Still looking up at her, he grinned. "Good night, Chyna."

"You, too."

"Will I see you Saturday night?" he asked.

Chyna quickly went through her plans. All she had

was that grand opening event, but that wouldn't last all day.

"Yes," she answered. "This time you get to pick the place. Just don't go overboard."

"Think paper napkins and peanut shells on the floor," he said.

"Now you're getting the hang of it," she laughed. She gave him a small wave before closing the window and pulling down the shade. She couldn't make herself step away from the window. Instead, she lifted the edge of the shade and peeked out, her eyes following Jared as he crossed the street and opened his car door. He stopped with one foot in the car and stared back at her building for a long moment before sliding behind the wheel. A second later, the headlights came on and the Mercedes pulled away from the curb.

Chyna was shocked at the sense of bereavement that came over her. What was happening to her? This was only their second date. Why did it feel as if a lightbulb had dimmed, and wouldn't get back to full wattage until Saturday?

"This is ridiculous," Chyna said, letting go of the window shade. She sat on the end table next to the window and expelled a sigh.

She was barreling full steam ahead toward a heap of trouble, and she couldn't do a single thing to stop it.

Chapter 10

Jared stood on the forty yard line with his arms crossed, a metal whistle resting between his lips. He tried to concentrate on the four college seniors running sprints between the hash marks, but his mind continued to bombard him with the image of Samantha and Carlos embracing, smiling into each other's eyes. Someone had left a copy of the celebrity magazine in the common area of the locker room, opened to an article that covered some charity event in Miami the two had attended over the weekend.

Anger and disgust burned hot in his gut as he recalled the contented bliss that was evident on both their faces. The unmistakable adoration as they gazed upon each other couldn't have been forged in the few months since he'd found Samantha and Carlos in bed together. It took time to build that kind of love.

Jared had often wondered how long their affair had

been going on behind his back. And how long it would have continued if they hadn't been caught.

He shook his head with a fierce curse.

Disregarding the stopwatch in his hand, Jared mentally counted down the seconds before blowing the whistle.

"Stop," he yelled. The guys abruptly halted their sprints.

Jared strolled up to the four players, trying like hell to keep his expression impassive. They looked ready to piss in their pants. Man, he remembered those days, jumping through hoops—literally—to impress the players and coaches. Willing to do just about anything to earn a spot on some team's roster.

After a lifetime of Pop Warner, high school and college football, knowing that your performance over a single week could decide whether you got to continue playing the game or hung up your shoulder pads forever; that was a lot for a twenty-one-year-old kid to handle.

Torrian walked up to him, carrying a clipboard and wearing an identical whistle attached to a teal-and-gray Sabers lanyard.

"How did this group do?" Torrian asked.

"Some had better numbers than others," Jared answered.

Torrian addressed the players. "You guys ready for The Wall?" He gestured to the twenty-five-foot cushioned wall with several ropes dangling from the top of it. Jared *hated* that damn wall, but he loved watching other guys fight with it.

As Torrian walked the group toward the apparatus, Jared headed for the Gatorade station. Randall was standing next to it, gulping down fluid from a paper cup.

"Nothing like tryout week," Randall said with a

wicked laugh. "I especially love seeing the cocky ones who've bought into all the hype from the sports analysts get what's coming to them. A Heisman trophy doesn't mean crap when you have three hundred pounds of pissed off linebacker charging after your ass."

"You want to see some real tears?" Jared grinned and nodded toward the back end of the field. "Torrian is taking the group I just worked with over The Wall."

"And today isn't even my birthday," Randall said with the excitement only one who'd suffered at the hands of The Wall could experience. "Hey." He nudged Jared's shoulder as they strolled across the practice field. "Did you end up going out with The Brain on Friday?"

"Don't call her that," Jared snapped.

"Why? That's her name."

"Her name is Chyna. And, yeah, we went out."

"And?" Randall asked when Jared didn't elaborate.

"And it's none of your business."

"Man, I know you're not holding out on me. I'm the one who told you to go after her in the first place."

"And when she blew me off you told me to go after another one," Jared reminded his teammate. "So, yeah, I'm holding out on you. Chyna and I had a good time. That's all you need to know."

Randall shook his head. "Dude, that's not even cool."

"Maybe if you went on your own date you wouldn't be so concerned about mine."

"Last date I had was with Big Bird and Elmo."

"Hard to compete." Jared grinned.

"That's nothing. I've got *Nemo and Friends on Ice* up next. Eat your heart out."

They stopped about ten yards back from The Wall and openly pointed and chuckled at the rookies who were literally brought to their knees by the grueling exercise.

With a twinge of unease, Jared noticed the cornerback from Rutgers lasted the longest.

He'd been surprised that the rookie had been brought in for tryouts. Everyone knew the Sabers were in the hunt for a new quarterback now that their star for the past nine seasons, Mark Landon, had decided to retire. Talk around camp had been that the Sabers would trade their first- and second-round draft picks in order to get a more experienced quarterback from one of the other teams, but Sabers upper management were playing their cards close to their chest. Not even the players knew what move they would make come Draft Day.

But there wasn't a single mock draft in the online fantasy sports arena that had the Sabers picking a cornerback, which made their choice to audition the player from Rutgers even more puzzling. Why not bring in a quarterback or maybe another running back to take the load off Cedric Reeves's shoulders? Hell, they'd just lost that bastard Carlos Garcia to the Colts. Why not try out a rookie tight end to fill his spot?

After another ten minutes of torturing the candidates, Torrian blew his whistle and called all eleven of the potential draft picks into a huddle.

Jared checked his watch. He had only a few minutes before he had to join the team in the media conference room. The rookies would be given a chance to shower then it was a bit of show-and-tell for the rest of the afternoon. A current player from every position would discuss their role on the team and give some insight into the Sabers organization.

"I'll meet you in the media room," Jared told Randall before heading toward the field house's exit. He pulled out his phone and called Chyna, but his call went to voice mail. He tried again with the same result before remembering that she was at work and probably couldn't take personal calls.

He wasn't used to dating a woman with a regular day job. Even though Samantha had a degree in finance, she hadn't held a job since finishing her internship back in their senior year at San Diego State. Once it was obvious that Jared would be drafted into the NFL, there was no need for her to work.

Jared suppressed the rage that flared at the thought of how Samantha had used him. He'd given that girl everything she could possibly want, and it hadn't been enough.

He pushed through the main building's double doors with a silent curse. He was done with this self-torture. He'd spent a decade of his life making sure Samantha wanted for nothing, and look at how she'd repaid him. He was done. Samantha had made her choice, and he was making his.

His cell phone rang, and Jared nearly dropped it in his haste to answer, but it wasn't Chyna's number on the screen.

"Yeah, Patrick," Jared answered with a terse breath.

"You can at least pretend you're happy to hear from me," his college buddy said.

"I thought—" hoped "—you were someone else."

"The growl kinda gave that away," Patrick said. "I'm just calling to tell you the Red Zone passed inspection. We are good to go, my man."

Jared's shoulders sagged with relief. "That's the kind of news I needed to hear today. Congratulations, man. Hey, is everything ready for Saturday? You need me to do anything?"

"It's all taken care of. Just be there by ten o'clock for the ribbon cutting. I've got a photographer from the *Post* coming."

"You *have* taken care of everything," Jared said, impressed. "I'll see you Saturday."

He disconnected Patrick's call and stared at the phone, willing it to ring with Chyna on the other end. It didn't.

Jared shook his head, unable to believe a woman whose name he didn't even know a week ago could have him staring at the phone like a love-struck teenager. Chyna was supposed to be only a distraction, someone to help get his mind off Samantha. But in just over seventy-two hours she'd become so much more than that. He couldn't get *her* off his mind. And the more he thought about her, the more he wanted to be with her.

Saturday night couldn't get here fast enough.

Chyna met up with Liani inside the marble-and-gold lobby of the Fifth Avenue building that housed her parents' eight-thousand-square-foot penthouse. Chyna turned right when they exited the building, heading for the subway, but Liani caught her by the elbow.

"This way," she said, nodding to a black Lincoln Town Car with tinted windows. "I figure since I'm staying here, I might as well take advantage of all the perks, right?"

When the Dixon family's personal driver pulled the Town Car in front of a handsome brownstone at the corner of 107th Street and Amsterdam Avenue, Chyna sent Liani a quizzical look. "Are you sure this is the right place? It doesn't look like a barbershop to me."

"This is it. The Red Zone." Liani pointed to a chrome-plated sign flanked on either side by three-feet-tall red-and-white barbershop spirals. They climbed out of the backseat with Liani leaving instructions for the driver to meet them back here in another two and a half hours.

"There's Kenya and Jamie," Chyna said, pointing

at two members of the Saberrettes squad who had just turned the corner.

"Hi, girlies," Kenya greeted. She motioned to Chyna's dress. "Look at you looking all *Project Runway.* Somebody's trying to land herself a man."

"From what I hear she already has," Jamie said. "I heard about you and Jared Dawson."

Chyna opened her mouth to respond, but Kenya cut her off. "You're dating Jared Dawson?" she asked, her pencil-thin brow arched in inquiry. Her joking tone had taken on a note of accusation. "I guess there are some perks to being just a choreographer. No one looks at you as if you're a gold digger since you're not in a Saberrette uniform."

"First of all, I didn't take this job to land a man," Chyna said. "And it's not really anyone's business what I'm doing with Jared."

"I agree," Liani said. "What Chyna and Jared do is no one else's business, except for mine since I'm her best friend. Now can we stop the chitchat and get to work." She pulled out her cell phone and scrolled through a list of messages. "According to Amy's email, we're meeting someone named Patrick. Go to the side entrance that's just off the alley."

The four of them walked around the side of the building. Chyna followed a few steps behind, trying to get a handle on her temper, burning slowly just beneath the surface.

Of all the things Kenya could have accused her of, being a gold digger was up there with mass murder. Chyna took care of herself. Always. She'd been schooled in the art of self-reliance years ago, and had worked her ass off to make sure she never had to depend on anyone else for her well-being.

She was not dating Jared for his money. If anything, his extravagant lifestyle had been more of a hindrance than a benefit to their…relationship, for lack of a better word. Chyna wasn't sure if she would call two and a half dates a relationship, but when they took place in the span of two and a half days, it deserved some kind of title.

She forced herself to shove Kenya's words out of her mind. She was here to support the Saberrettes and get an idea of the type of work they did outside of the stadium. She would not let Kenya Simmons get to her.

"This must be it." Liani knocked on the side door, but with the music blasting on the other side, Chyna doubted anyone would hear. "Is this a barbershop or a dance club?" her friend asked.

The door opened and a handsome guy with wire-rimmed glasses greeted them. "Oh, great. You're just in time. Come on in." He gestured for them to follow him into a small room with shelving on either side of a narrow walkway. They were stacked with white towels, toilet tissue and boxes with pictures of little black combs on the outside, evidence that it was, indeed, a barbershop.

He glanced back over his shoulder. "The deejay just started up, and we're about to have the first door-prize drawing. I'd like you all to take turns drawing the names." He abruptly stopped and turned. "Hey, aren't you all supposed to be in uniforms?"

"Give us a minute," Liani said. "Is there somewhere we can store our bags?"

He gestured to an empty shelf a few feet away. "You can put them right there. The door leading to this room stays locked, so everything will be safe."

Chyna stood to the side as, like synchronized swimmers, the three women simultaneously stripped out of their warm-up suits, revealing the barely there teal-and-metallic-gray uniforms underneath. Each squad member stuffed their warm-up suit into their personalized Saberrettes duffel bags and placed them on the empty shelf.

Liani tapped Patrick on the chin. "Close your mouth, honey. There's no need to drool."

One by one they filed out of the back room and entered the main area of the barbershop. Chyna was the last out. She walked through the door and came face-to-face with Jared.

"The Saberrettes are here."

Jared heard Patrick's voice coming from somewhere behind him, but his business partner could have been yelling "fire" for all he cared. As he stared at Chyna standing there in a hot pink dress that was holding on to her curves for dear life, he had a hard time focusing on anything else.

Her gray eyes widened in astonishment. "What are *you* doing here?"

Jared shook his head, trying to get his bearings straight. "This is my place," he finally answered. "Well, partly mine. I'm an investor. I knew the Saberrettes would be here, but I didn't know you were joining them."

He glanced at her face, but couldn't keep his eyes from traveling back to the luscious breasts that were deliciously displayed in the deep V of her dress.

"Liani invited me to tag along so I can get a sense of how the Saberrettes function outside of their normal dancing duties."

"Chyna!" Jared heard one of the other girls call her name.

"I've got to go," she said, stepping around him.

As he watched her stroll over to where the other dance

squad members stood, Jared had a hard time reconciling the woman he'd just spoken to with the one he'd spent the day with last Sunday. The makeup, fancy hair and clingy dress were such a contrast to the ponytail and clean, fresh face that had greeted him at the park.

As turned on as he was by how incredible she looked right now, Jared acknowledged that he was just as attracted to the girl without all the bells and whistles.

The Saberrette with the blond hair pulled a slip of paper from the mesh steel drum Patrick had set up in the middle of the barbershop, and called a name for the first of four one-hundred-dollar gift certificates that would be given away as door prizes. The winner ran up and gave her a hug, then quickly moved to do the same with the other cheerleaders *and* their choreographer.

Jared's back stiffened and his hands instinctively clenched into fists. He didn't like the precedents that move set. He had no doubt that every winner would now follow in hugging all of the Saberrettes and Chyna, and Jared was fairly certain he would beat the hell out of any man who wrapped his arms around Chyna again.

The cheerleaders surrounded the winner, but before the photographer could snap their picture Liani gestured for Chyna to join them. She hesitated for a moment before scooting way too close to the guy who'd won the door prize.

A mother and two small boys came up to Jared and asked for his autograph, pulling his attention from what was transpiring in the center of the barbershop. Jared scribbled on the football and headed for the crowded lobby area to greet more patrons.

Patrick's promotional efforts had paid off better than either of them had expected. There had been a steady flow of people in and out of the barbershop all day. The demographic included varied ages and races, but the crowd was predominately male, a fact that sent his blood pressure spiking as he became aware of all the eyes on Chyna.

He didn't like it. Not at all.

Jared knew he was being ridiculous. After only two dates he had no claims on Chyna. Yet he couldn't help the possessiveness that stalked through him and demanded he snatch her away from all these leering eyes.

Jared had done the knockout gorgeous girlfriend routine before. He'd been proud to flaunt Samantha on his arm, knowing other men envied him. Until she'd been stolen away. He refused to go through that pain again.

Liani Dixon drew the second door prize, and once again, the winner used the opportunity to score hugs. Again, Chyna was invited to join the squad as they crowded together for a group picture, but this time Chyna stood immediately to the winner's left. When the guy put his arm around her waist and rested his palm on her hip, Jared saw red.

He started straight for the Saberrettes, who were rustling their glittery pom-poms and posing for pictures. He caught Chyna by the elbow and half guided, half dragged her to the break room behind the bar.

"Jared, what are you doing?" she balked.

He ignored her question as he pulled his wallet from his back pocket and started peeling away hundred-dollar bills. "How much are you being paid to be here?"

"Excuse me? I'm not being—"

"Dammit," he cut her off. "This is all I have on me." Jared handed her five hundred dollars. "This is part of the money for the vet bill. When I pick you up tonight I'll give you the rest of it along with whatever consultant fee you charged Patrick for being here today. Just don't go back out there."

Her shocked expression was quickly replaced with outrage. "First of all, I'm not being paid to be here. I came to offer support to the girls on the squad."

"Is that your special offering-support dress?"

She looked down at the silky dress that clung to her body and stopped just above the knee. "What's wrong with my dress?"

"Not a damn thing. That's the problem."

"Jared, I don't have time for this. Technically, I'm working."

She tried to push past him, but Jared caught her arm. He pointed toward the main area of the barbershop. "That isn't 'working,' it's…being fantasy material for some guy's wet dream."

"Do you really think the guys out there are paying any attention to me when there are three cheerleaders wearing the equivalent of bathing suits? I don't see you demanding any of the Saberrettes cover up."

"I don't give a damn what they do. I'm not going out with the other girls."

She looked down at where he still held her. "Jared, if you don't let go of me right now, I swear I'm going to hurt you."

She yanked her arm away and headed for the door. She stopped with her hand on the handle and swung around to face him again. Jared could feel the heat from her blistering, defiant stare. She stomped back to him and stepped right up into his face.

"Let's get one thing straight. You have no say in what I put on this body, you got that? And my being out there with the rest of the dance squad is a part of my job. If you have a problem with it, then you have a problem with me. Either figure out a way to deal with it or find someone else to go on this date tonight." She poked his chest with her finger. "I told you once before that I take care of myself." Her eyes were steely, her voice cold as ice. "Don't you *ever* think you can come in and dictate what I do."

Turning on her heel, she stalked out of the break room.

Chapter 11

Jared clutched the cellophane-wrapped tulips in one hand and used the other to hit the doorbell on Chyna's building. He buzzed once, then again. He was about to hit it a third time when he heard, "Who is it?" come through the electronic keypad.

Jared took a deep breath, thought about heading back to his car, then manned up and said, "It's me," into the buzzer.

He was met with silence on the other end.

"Chyna?" Jared called into the speaker.

Two minutes later, the building's front door opened and she came out wearing a pair of sweatpants and an oversized "I Dance, Therefore I Jam" T-shirt. Jared was just as turned on as when he'd first spotted her in that revealing dress.

He bowed his head and held up the flowers. "I heard my evil twin showed up at the Red Zone earlier today and got all jealous and bossy with you. I killed him and threw his body in the East River on my way over here."

There was a long moment of tense silence where he felt true fear that he may have ruined things with her forever. But then a burst of sweet laughter brought his head up, and the smile on Chyna's face melted away some of his anxiety. Despite her amused reaction, Jared knew he had a long way to go to make up for the way he'd behaved today.

"I guess I can't hold you accountable for your evil twin's actions," she said, taking the flowers and bringing them to her nose. "As long as you know I won't put up with the macho crap your evil twin tried to pull today."

"I really am sorry, Chyna. I'm not usually the jealous type, but…" He glanced at her, then away. "My ex, Samantha…she would strut around in sexy dresses and high heels, and I loved it. I loved knowing that other guys envied what I had. But then…"

"Then you lost her," she said with such gentle understanding, Jared's throat tightened.

"Yeah. As much as I try to deny it, I'm still kind of messed up over what happened with Sam. I didn't mean to take it out on you."

"You told me the two of you had been together for ten years, Jared. It's not something you're going to easily get over."

"That's the thing," he said. "Since the moment I met you, I've hardly thought about Sam. I thought it would be years before I stopped thinking about her every day, remembering what we had. But it hasn't been that way. You're so good for me, Chyna."

He reached over and captured her hand within his. "I'm so sorry for being such a jackass. What can I do to convince you to go on our date?"

She hesitated a moment, then after a deep breath, said, "I've been thinking about what happened today, and it just confirmed what I already knew. This thing between us will never work."

Panic gripped his chest. "Why do we all of a sudden not work?"

"It's not all of a sudden. From the minute I agreed to have dinner with you, I've been trying to figure out if I lost my mind. I should have known better."

Confusion crippled his thoughts. Cupping her chin, he searched her face, trying to figure out what had gone wrong. "Chyna, I don't understand. What's the problem?"

She jerked her chin from his grasp and twisted away from him. When she turned back, resentment clouded her eyes. "The problem is that you thought you could just make everything better by shoving money into my hands today. The problem is that I don't want to invite you into my apartment because I'm ashamed of how small and cramped it is. I'm too embarrassed to let you see where I live, Jared. *Now* do you understand?" she said, her voice cracking on the last word.

She wrapped her arms around her middle, closing him off.

Jared took a tentative step forward, but managed to stop himself from touching her. "You don't have to be ashamed of anything," he said in a quiet voice.

"That's just it. I have *never* been ashamed of where I live. I'm proud of it." She looked up at him, her eyes twin pools of self-disgust. "Do you know how hard I've had to work just to be able to afford this dingy little apart-ment? And then you come along with your millions and I'm too ashamed for you to even see it."

"Do you think I'm going to judge you?" he asked,

more hurt than he could verbalize that she would think so little of him.

"I don't know. I just…" She shook her head. "We're different, Jared. I may play around in your world, but I'm not a part of it and I never will be. And, you know what? I'm fine with that. I don't need fame and fortune. I work hard and I get to dance. That's good enough for me."

"Why would you think it isn't good enough for me?" he asked. "I love that you work hard, and that you're independent, and strong and beautiful. I wouldn't care if you lived in a cardboard box." He paused. "Okay, maybe I'd have a problem with a cardboard box."

That got the reaction he was hoping for. She smiled.

Jared captured her shoulders and gave them a gentle, reassuring squeeze. "I would never think less of you because of where you live. I'm not that kind of guy, Chyna." He took her chin in his hands and tilted her face up. With all the contrition he could muster, he said, "And I'm sorry for the way I behaved today. I was out of line."

"You understand why I couldn't accept the money, right?"

"Yes," he answered. "As much as I wanted to drag you out of there, I get why you reacted the way you did. I respect you so much for being as strong as you are, Chyna. I really do. I'm just not used to a woman who's so sure of herself."

"It's the only way I know how to be. So, if this…"

"Relationship," Jared offered when she seemed at a loss for words.

"Relationship." She nodded. "If it's going to continue, you have to accept that I take care of myself, Jared."

"Accepted," he said. "Now, can we please get on with

this date? I promised to show you how to have fun, and I'm ready to get started."

Her mouth dipped in a contemplative frown before she said, "I already told Abby I would fill in for her. She sprained her ankle and can't teach her salsa class."

"I can come with you to the dance studio," he said.

She eyed him with a skeptical frown. "You don't want to spend your evening watching a bunch of rhythmless people dance the salsa. Trust me on this."

Jared grinned. "Maybe not, but I'll enjoy watching their teacher shake her sexy hips." He leaned over and rested his forehead against hers, breathing in her clean scent. "Please, let me come with you. I want to see you in action."

Jared could see the indecision playing behind her eyes. He tipped his mouth down in hopes of making the decision for her. He caught her bottom lip between his teeth and gently nipped and sucked her sweetness into his mouth. Chyna pulled away with a soft moan.

"Okay, you convinced me," she said. "Just promise me you'll behave yourself."

"My sister had this sticker on her bedroom door that said 'Women who behave themselves rarely have fun.' I think that's true for men, too." She didn't respond, just gave him a look that said she wasn't budging from her request.

"Fine," Jared grunted. "I'll behave myself."

Two hours later, as he leaned his head against the wall at the Borne Academy of Dance where Chyna volunteered, Jared was having the hardest time getting one particular part of his body to behave. From the moment Chyna sauntered across the hardwood floors and started shaking her hips, he'd been in a constant state of arousal.

Her hips rotated in a hypnotic rhythm that had blood

rushing to his groin. Jared couldn't pry his eyes from her body's sensual motion. She was mesmerizing, swaying back and forth in the sexiest, most tantalizing way.

She turned her back to the class and faced the mirrored wall. She flashed him a quick glance out of the corner of her eye and grinned.

"Okay, class," she said, all business again. "The basic salsa step is one of the simplest in all of dance. Once you master it, you'll have a foundation for learning all the other steps." Chyna held her hands up in front of her as if she were holding on to an imaginary partner. "We start with the left foot," she said as she took a step forward. "One, two, three. Back. Five, six, seven. Stop."

She turned to the class of eight. "Now you try."

Jared could barely contain his laughter as he watched the students trip over their own feet as they attempted to mimic Chyna's fluid dance steps. She made it look effortless. Effortless and erotic.

Chyna guided each student, giving extra attention to those who were having the hardest time with the simple dance move.

"To do the cross body lead, we start with the basic step, but on six and seven, the right foot comes around."

Jared's entire focus remained on Chyna. He could watch her glide across the floor for hours, her tight, sweet ass shimmying from side to side. He pressed his head against the wall and shut his eyes tight against the groan that nearly escaped. God, he wanted this woman. Witnessing her in action for the past hour, it was all too easy to imagine her moving the same way. Naked. In bed. Her body hovering over his as she pumped up and down.

Jared moaned.

When the class ended, he remained in the spot he'd occupied for the past hour and a half, not rising until the room was cleared of all students. Chyna walked over to him, dabbing her cheeks with the towel she'd slung around her neck.

"Not the way you expected to spend your Saturday evening, right?"

He trailed his eyes down her body in a slow perusal, from the top of her head to tips of her toes that looked amazing in her strappy high heels.

"Watching you move your body the way you did? I can't think of a better way to spend my Saturday evening." He paused, staring at her with a look that made his intent unmistakable. "Actually, I can think of one better way."

Her creamy brown skin instantly blushed.

"Sorry the class ran a little long, but I wanted to make sure they mastered the basic step," she said. "Since it was the last class of the night, I figured I could just lock up whenever."

"You won't get any complaints from me," he said. "I loved watching you dance. I can tell how much you enjoy it."

"I really do," she said. "Even when I have to teach the same thing over and over and over. This class was slower to catch on than most, but I think I left them in pretty good shape for Abby. She's the usual salsa instructor."

"What classes do you teach?"

"Jazz and hip hop for eight- to twelve-year-olds. They retain the info better than the adults. I sometimes teach the tango as well, but not this year."

"Well, that's too bad, because the tango is what I want to learn," Jared said. She shook her head, but he countered with a nod as he wrapped one arm around her waist and captured her hand in his other. "You promised me a dance lesson. I'm collecting."

"You don't want me to teach you the tango tonight. I'm all sweaty."

His brow hiked. "And the thought of you all sweaty is supposed to be a turnoff?" He wrapped an arm around her waist and pulled her close. "Woman, I've been dreaming of getting you hot and sweaty for days."

"Does that line really work?" Chyna choked on a laugh.

"You tell me," he returned with a wicked grin.

She wiggled out of his hold and sauntered over to the small square table that held an iPod and speaker system. She lifted the iPod from the resting dock, found what she was looking for, and seconds later sultry music flowed from the speakers.

She turned to him, and with a slow smile creeping across her lips, crooked her finger. Jared made it across the room so fast he was pretty sure he'd been airborne for a few seconds.

Chyna took his right hand and placed it around her waist, then held up his left hand at shoulder level. "So, Mr. Dawson, how much experience do you have with ballroom dancing?"

"None." He shook his head. "But I'm a quick learner, especially when I want to impress my teacher."

Her lips curved in the kind of smile that made him forget his first name.

"Let's see what you've got," she said. "Since I'm the expert here, it's only right that I lead."

"I'm happy to follow you wherever you want to take me," he said, fitting his palm at the small of her back and pulling her more securely against him.

"Are you ready to tango?"

"Do I get to keep you this close to me?"

"Oh, yeah." Her voice was husky, raspy. "This dance

requires us to stand very close." To drive the point home she pulled him flush against her. Jared's entire body ignited.

"The tango is all about attitude and rhythm," Chyna said. She closed her eyes and let her head fall back. "Let the music seep into your soul." She lifted her head and her gray eyes stared directly into his. "Follow me," she urged as she took a step back.

They moved slowly across the dance floor, her steps fluid. Sensual. Chyna counted the beats as she guided him around the room.

"Now stop," she said. Bringing their movements to an abrupt halt. "Now I draw my leg up, like this." She glided her leg up his thigh, hooking her foot behind his knee. "And you counter by putting your leg between mine."

Just like that, his cock stiffened to the point of pain. Chyna's breath hitched at the contact, but she didn't pull away. Her eyelids lowered and her breathing followed, coming in soft pants.

"Hold my waist like this," she instructed, placing his hand on her flat stomach. Then she spun around, molding her back to his front before lowering herself on an erotic slide down his body.

Lesson over.

Jared twirled her around and crushed his mouth to hers. He lifted her and she wrapped her legs around his waist.

"Jared, wait," she said against his lips.

He ground his stiffening erection against her hot center. "You don't really want me to," he said.

She tore her mouth from his. "You're right, I don't," she said. She looked him in the eyes. "But we can't do this here."

"Then where?" he asked. "Because no matter what, in ten minutes I'm going to be inside of you."

A jolt of need shot like an arrow down Chyna's spine, settling in a pool of desire between her thighs. Blood pounded in her ears and her heart raced with the arousal Jared's hot promise created.

"I don't live too far from here," she said.

She felt his muscles stiffen against her. He took a step back, his intense gaze boring into hers with a combination of inquiry and lust. Instinctively, her tongue darted out of her mouth and wet her lips. Jared's gaze zeroed in on her mouth and his breathing slowed, his chest rising and falling with measured breaths as he continued to stare at her lips.

"I'm giving you one minute to change your mind."

She shook her head. "I won't change my mind. I want you."

He pulled in a deep breath and crushed his mouth against hers in a swift kiss. They quickly shut off the lights and Chyna locked up the studio.

The drive from the dance school to her apartment was only a few minutes, but felt like an eternity. Now that she'd made the decision to take this momentous step, her body shivered with eager anticipation of everything Jared had to offer.

He pulled up to the curb and shut off the engine, but didn't make a move to exit the car. His hands tightened on the steering wheel. "I need to take a minute to calm down. If I don't, I'm going to jump all over you the minute we get inside."

His visible struggle fascinated her. His hands, jaw and eyes all clenched tight as his chest expanded with another intake of air.

"Jared?" Chyna waited for him to look over at her before she continued. "I kinda want you to jump me as soon as we get inside."

His eyes narrowed with smoldering need. Without another word, they both rushed out of the car and up the stairs. Anticipation turned her fingers to jelly as she fumbled to open the door to her apartment. As soon as there were inside, Chyna tossed the keys and flung her arms around his neck.

Jared picked her up, wrapping her legs around his waist. One hand skimmed her hip and thigh while the other gripped her butt, clutching her to him. He pinned her to the door, going for the hem of her shirt while he assaulted her with bruising kisses along her neck and collarbone.

Chyna pulled the T-shirt off and threw it to the floor. Her skin tingled with delicious anticipation as Jared's head plunged south. He dove for her breasts, nipping and licking and sucking through her purple lace bra. One hand snaked up her spine to the single eyehook, which he released with an expertise Chyna didn't want to think about.

She didn't want to think about anything but the feel of his tongue against her sensitive, long-neglected nipples. He switched from one to the other, drawing hot, wet circles around the turgid nub before drawing it into his warm mouth and tugging.

She cried out, arching her back against the door.

Jared tucked one arm under her behind and gripped her back with the other as he carried her from the living room to her bedroom.

"Summer, move," he said, and for the first time Chyna registered her dog yipping and scampering around Jared's feet. As he placed her none too gently in the center of the bed, Chyna forgot all about Summer.

"God, that's sexy," he said, staring down at her.

"What?" Chyna asked, pushing up on her elbows.

"You. Lying there topless."

He pulled his shirt over his head, but when his hand went for his waist, Chyna stopped him.

"I'll do that," she said. She sat up and unbuttoned his jeans. With some effort, she tugged the zipper down his rigid fly. Together they both pushed the jeans and black silk boxers from his hips. His erection sprang forward, thicker and bigger than she was expecting.

Chyna experienced a twinge of apprehension. It had been a while since she'd done this. She wasn't sure her body could accept all of him without being torn in two.

Jared tenderly caressed her cheek and her anxiety floated away on a wave of trust and longing. She wrapped her hand around his pulsing erection, but he quickly removed it.

"No." He shook his head. "I doubt I'll last more than five minutes as it is." He gestured with his chin. "Lie back."

Chyna did as she was told, scooting back until her head met the headboard. Jared knelt beside her on the bed and hooked his thumbs at the waistband of her black leggings. His fingers left a stream of scorching need as they trailed along her thighs and legs. He laid his palm flat, just above the edge of her lace underwear, then glided his hand up her stomach to the valley between her breasts. He bent over her and his tongue seared a path along her abdomen, leaving a hot, moist trail in its wake.

He gripped her boy-cut panties and pulled them from her hips and down her legs. Chyna kicked the underwear away, and her body instantly blushed at the realization that she lay completely naked before him.

"Don't you dare," Jared said when she went to cover herself.

Reaching over the side of the bed, he pulled his wallet from the back pocket of his jeans and drew out a condom. He ripped the package open and quickly covered himself. Then he braced a hand on each side of her head and lowered his body.

Summer yelped.

Chyna looked over to find her dog on the pillow next to her.

"I can't do this with her watching us," Chyna said.

"She doesn't know what we're doing," Jared reasoned, trailing his tongue along her bare shoulder.

Chyna tried to forget about Summer's watchful eyes as Jared's huge body hovered above her. He went for her neck, nipping just below her ear. Chyna tensed as she felt the blunt head of his erection probe at her center.

Before he could penetrate her, he drew back with a frustrated grunt.

"Yeah, okay. This exhibitionist thing isn't working for me, either. It's like having your kid watch you have sex."

He rolled off of her and scooped Summer from the bed. Scratching behind the dog's perked ears, Jared said, "I will buy you every doggie treat in Manhattan if you be a good girl and don't make any noise."

Chyna couldn't help but laugh. Wasn't he the same person who'd made fun of her for talking about her dog as if she were a real person?

Jared opened the bedroom door and placed Summer on the other side of it. As he strode back to the bed, Chyna's amusement swiftly turned to arousal as she took in the corded muscles of his sinewy thighs, arms and stomach. He was strength and power and maleness. A captivating combination that made her skin prickle with awareness and her stomach clench with expectation.

"Now," Jared murmured, resuming his position above her. "Where were we?"

As he lowered himself, Chyna had a feeling she was embarking on one of the most pleasurable rides of her life. With the long, wet swipe of Jared's tongue across her nipple, she knew it as fact.

He levered himself up on one arm and advanced on her breasts with single-minded determination, laving the rigid peaks with his tongue and sucking with just enough pressure to drive her out of her mind. Chyna's stomach clenched with each sinful pull, her hand snaking up Jared's spine to his head, holding it more firmly to her breast.

As he continued to worship her with his mouth, one errant finger skimmed its way down her taut stomach to the moist curls between her legs. With deliberate slowness, he trailed his finger through the slick folds, finding his way to the knot of pulsing nerves at her cleft and rubbing with gentle pressure.

Chyna burrowed her head in the pillow, staring up at the ceiling as she tried to concentrate on the chaotic mass of sensation shooting from points along her body. From her breasts that were still held prisoner by his seeking tongue to the spot between her legs that vibrated with need. She was so close her entire being quaked with it, her body trembling with anticipatory pleasure, staggering on the brink of fulfillment but not quite there.

In an act of supreme mercy, Jared put her out of her misery, slipping two fingers inside of her and bringing her to a swift, shattering climax. Before she had the chance to come down from the sensual high, he removed his fingers from her body and replaced them with his thick erection. His arms straining on either side of her head, he rocked back and forth with powerful, fluid strokes, filling her with every inch of him before pulling almost completely out.

Loud, sharp gasps escaped her throat with each thrust of his hips, filling the room with the music of their lovemaking. Chyna closed her eyes and lost herself in the hypnotic rhythm, undulating her hips to meet him stroke for stroke.

Without warning he increased the tempo, plunging deep and swift, in and out, taking her higher and faster toward the climax she knew awaited her just on the other side. Chyna gripped his backside and pulled him tighter against her, sinking her fingers into his flesh.

Jared groaned deep in his throat. The corded muscles of his neck stood out in stark relief as he started pumping with fierce, maddening strokes. Over and over and over. He plunged into her body, circling his hips and driving her head against the headboard with the force of his thrusts.

A burst of sensation ricocheted throughout her bloodstream as she came. The pleasure was pure and explosive, making her body hum with satisfaction.

Jared's sweat-slicked chest crushed her, but Chyna was too tired—too totally, utterly, deliciously spent—to complain. Her rolled off her and collapsed on the bed, expelling an exhausted sigh.

Chyna threw a languid arm over her eyes. "I've never had movie sex before," she said between labored breaths. "I should have known I'd get it with you."

"Movie sex?"

"Yeah," she said, turning over and resting her head in

her upturned palm. "You know, with clothes flying everywhere and multiple orgasms. It's only in the movies that people have that kind of sex."

His eyebrow tipped up in the sexiest way imaginable. "Is that what you think? That it only happens in the movies?" He reached over and pulled her on top of him. "Give me a few minutes of recovery time, sweetheart. Hollywood's got nothing on what I'm going to do to you."

Chapter 12

"What time does your class end?"

Jared fitted the phone more securely between his ear and shoulder. He switched from Sports Talk TV to ESPN, trying to decide which had the better pre-Draft coverage.

"I have a hip-hop class in five minutes, and then I'm done for the day," Chyna answered.

"Will you come over?"

"But it's Draft Day. I thought you'd be watching it at the Sabers compound."

"Nah," Jared said. "I'm not up for a crowd. I'd rather be with you."

She paused, then said, "That's so sweet."

He lowered his voice. "Sweet doesn't describe what I have in mind."

A half hour later, there was a buzz from the concierge desk. "Mr. Dawson, there is a Miss McCrea here to see you."

Jared told the concierge to let her up and raced for the door. He was waiting at the elevator when it opened.

"What happened to your class?" he asked as soon as Chyna stepped into the hall.

"Canceled." She dropped her bag just inside the door and took his face into her hands. "The instructor caught a case of the stomach flu. It seemed to have miraculously gone away on the subway ride over here."

She attacked his mouth as they both stripped out of their clothes.

Twenty sweaty, exhausting minutes later, Jared lay completely spent, staring at the recessed lights of his living room's high ceilings. They'd tried to make it to the sofa, but only managed to get as far as the faux fur rug before turning each other inside out.

The woman had an insatiable appetite, which was just fine with him. He'd love nothing more than to spend the next seventy-two hours naked and exhausted and wrapped up with Chyna.

She rolled off him and turned, fitting her back against him and drawing his arm across her waist. Jared spooned more firmly against her moist, smooth skin. He trailed his hand from her shoulder to her hip, then back up to cup her breast. Teasing her nipple with his thumb, he nudged the hair away from her neck and gave her a quick love bite.

"Was that movie sex?" he whispered against her neck.

"Oh, yeah. Completely X-rated."

With a deep chuckle, Jared pushed up from the floor and went into the bedroom, pulling the down comforter from the bed. He walked back up the hallway and stopped short at the gorgeous display of firm breasts and delicately rounded hips standing in the middle of his living room.

God, she was divine. With her long, wavy hair and

heart-stopping curves, all she needed was a half shell and she would be Botticelli's perfect caramel-colored Venus.

She noticed him and smiled, not displaying even a hint of the embarrassment she'd shown when he'd first stripped her clothes off last Saturday night.

"The draft is about to start," she said. "Are we watching in here or the media room?"

"You choose," Jared said. "As long as we watch it naked, I don't care."

Jared grabbed a bottle of wine and brought it into the media room. He sat in the center chair and opened his arms for Chyna to join him. She snuggled into the cradle of his arms, her skin still warm and damp from their floor sex.

Her bare hip rubbed against him and his body instantly responded, swelling to almost a full erection. Chyna peered at him over her shoulder.

"Are you sure you can handle naked TV?"

"I'll handle it…or die trying," he gasped, willing his body to calm down. He powered up the entertainment system and adjusted the volume. "There's still another twenty minutes before the first draft pick is announced."

"Any idea who is going first?"

"There's always a pool—completely under the table, of course—betting on which guy will go first, but no one ever really knows other than the team that's on the clock."

"You ever win the pool?"

"I don't bet, sweetheart."

She twisted around to look at him. "Why not?"

Jared debated how much he should tell her. Only his closest friends and a few people in the Sabers organization knew about his gambling issue, but his gut told him he could trust Chyna.

"I got into some trouble a few years back," he said. Then he clarified, "I bet on a couple of games."

"I would think that would be against the rules," she said.

"Oh, it is," Jared huffed out a humorless laugh. "But rules aren't always followed. Sabers upper management decided not to report me to the league if I agreed never to gamble again."

"You were lucky."

"I was damn lucky." He nodded. "I miss the excitement of waiting for a bet to pay off, but it's not worth losing my career. I've found other ways to create the adrenaline rush."

"Really?" she asked, snuggling against what had turned into a full-blown erection.

"Oh, yeah," Jared said. He shifted her around and drew her more firmly onto his lap, hooking an arm under each knee so that she straddled him.

"Jared," Chyna gasped. "What are you doing?"

"Wait a second." He clutched her waist. "I'll show you."

He took her hard and fast, plunging high and deep, bringing her to a swift and shattering orgasm. After the quickest, most erotic shower of their lives, Jared settled back into the buttery soft chair and pulled Chyna back onto his lap. Against his wishes, they were both wearing clothes, though the sight of her in his T-shirt and boxer shorts was almost as much of a turn-on as seeing her naked. Almost.

"So, when do the Sabers get to choose?" she asked, reaching over and grabbing a handful of popcorn she'd popped from the bowl. She stretched her hand over her shoulder to feed him a few pieces of popcorn, and Jared realized he could live in this moment for the rest of his life.

Never in all the time he and Samantha had been together had he felt so at peace just *being*. In only a few short weeks, he and Chyna had found a level of comfort that he'd never experienced with any other woman, even one he'd given ten years of his life to.

"The Sabers have the twenty-sixth spot."

"Why so late?"

"That's the way the draft works," he answered with a shrug. "Your positioning is based on your previous season record. The team with the worst record picks first, and the Super Bowl champs pick last. Unless a team has traded their draft pick, either to get a player on another team's squad or to move farther up in the draft."

Which is what everyone had speculated the Sabers would do in order to get a new quarterback, but Jared had yet to hear insider information on how upper management would proceed in today's draft. He'd tried to pull some info out of Torrian, but his friend wasn't talking.

They sat through the first five draft picks, which were all as predicted by the dozens of mock drafts posed by football analysts. Seeing the excitement on the young players' faces brought back memories of his own draft day. It was pure bliss for those picked early, but could be agony for the players waiting in the green room for their names to be called.

Watching the clock tick down the five minutes the Seattle Seahawks had to make their selection, Jared nuzzled the soft, pliant skin along Chyna's jawline, breathing in her unique scent.

"How were your earlier dance classes, before you got that nasty stomach flu?" he murmured against her neck.

"They were fine," she answered without much enthusiasm.

"You don't sound as if they were fine."

She shook her head, and with a deep sigh, said, "I found out today that the owners have decided to sell the school."

"The economy?" he asked.

"That may have factored into it, but I think they're just ready to retire. Mrs. Borne said they're moving to New Mexico to be closer to their grandchildren." She heaved a melancholy sigh. "My heart breaks for the girls in my class. I didn't have a place where I could take free lessons when I was a kid. I worked like crazy, doing odd jobs to scrape up the money for dance school. I hate the thought of those girls having to do the same."

He kissed her behind the ear. "Hopefully the next owners will keep the free lessons going."

"I hope so. If they're even able to sell the school, that is. It won't be easy to find a buyer in this economic climate."

"Maybe you should buy it," Jared urged.

"Right," Chyna snorted. "As my mother says, 'I don't have a money tree, just a fake ficus.' And I don't even have that. Summer ate all the leaves off the one plant I tried to keep at my apartment." She fitted herself more securely against his chest. "I'll just keep my thoughts positive and hope for the best. Maybe someone will see worth in it."

Jared ran a hand up and down her arm, mentally researching the contacts he had that could look into purchasing the dance school. Probably the real estate agent who had helped to find the building they had renovated for the Red Zone.

Buying the studio was a no-brainer, despite the fact

that he knew zero about owning a dance school. It wouldn't be the first venture he'd invested in to help out family and friends. Some had turned into a huge waste of money, but others, like the karate studio he'd financially backed for one of the guys on his high school football team and the yogurt shop he'd funded for his cousin, had turned a nice profit. So far, the Red Zone looked as if it would fall into the profitable category, too.

He wasn't looking to make any money from buying the dance school for Chyna. Just the chance to see the smile on her face when he presented it to her would be payment enough.

Damn, he'd nearly forgotten the gift he'd scored for her.

"Speaking of dancing," Jared opened. "I heard there was some fancy dance troupe at the Met tonight."

Chyna twisted, looking at him with guarded excitement in her eyes. "It is not just *any* dance troupe playing at the Met tonight. It's the Kirov Ballet, one of the oldest and most famous Russian ballet companies, and their one-night-only performance has been sold out for months. You do *not* have tickets," she stated.

Jared didn't respond, just continued to stare at the television, his mouth tipping up in a smile.

"Jared," she said with a warning tone.

"I'll pick you up at six."

Chyna's eyes widened with pure delight. He burst out laughing at her excited squeal.

"This is amazing," she squealed. "I'm considering this an early birthday gift."

"You have a birthday coming up? When?"

"Next Wednesday."

"Hmm…" He pressed a kiss to the top of her hand.

"That gives me a week and a half to figure out some way to celebrate."

"The ballet tickets are more than enough. Really, Jared, you have no idea how much this means to me." She rewarded him with a kiss that made him wish they were naked again. God, his body couldn't get enough of this woman.

She twisted back around and faced the TV again, bringing both his hands around and settling them on her stomach.

"Hey." She nudged his shoulder and pointed to the screen. "The Sabers are up next."

The NFL commissioner made his way to the podium.

"With the twenty-sixth pick in this year's draft, the New York Sabers select Delonte Cannon from Rutgers University."

There was a mixture of cheers and boos from the crowd at Madison Square Garden, which boasted a large number of Sabers fans. Jared hardly registered the noise. Panic struck his chest like a bolt of lightning, the instant shock rendering him speechless.

The Sabers had just used their valuable first-round draft pick to acquire a cornerback. *His* position.

"Is he good?" Chyna asked, oblivious to the storm that was churning in his gut.

"Yeah," Jared murmured. "He's good." He tapped her on the knee and gave her back a gentle nudge. "Can you let me up? I need to go to the bathroom."

Chyna scooted off his lap, but before he could walk away, she caught his arm. "Hey, are you okay?" she asked. "You look…I don't know…off."

"I'm good," Jared lied, bending down and placing a kiss on her nose. "You need me to bring you anything?"

"Just you," she answered, returning his kiss.

Jared headed for his bedroom, closing the door behind him as he pulled up Torrian's phone number on his cell. Pacing the floor in front of his bed, Jared tried to wrap his head around the message the Sabers' upper management had sent with that draft pick.

As soon as the call connected, Jared spit out in a fierce whisper, "What the hell is going on?"

"Just calm down," Torrian urged.

"Why should I when one of my best friends didn't bother to tell me my job was in jeopardy? You could have given me a heads-up, Wood."

"Look, man, we shouldn't even be discussing this. I'm already in a tough spot when it comes to still being so tight with both you and Cedric. There's an invisible line between coaches and players that you're not supposed to cross. You know that."

"Yeah, I know," Jared growled into the phone. He ran an agitated hand down his face as he continued to trek across the carpet. "I just didn't think I'd have to compete for my own damn job," he said.

"Your job is secure," Torrian reasoned. "Do you really think they would replace a veteran player with your numbers with a rookie fresh out of college? This was an investment in the future of the team. Delonte Cannon is going to be a great addition to the Sabers secondary in a few seasons and you'll be there to groom him. End of story."

"Yeah, if that's what you say."

"Don't worry about this, Jared. Just make sure you're at the top of your game when training camp starts in a few weeks."

"I always am," Jared said before he hung up.

He took a moment to calm himself down. Torrian was right; the Sabers were likely just planning for the

future. Jared had witnessed Delonte Cannon in action
during tryout week. The kid was a natural, with the type
of raw athletic ability that made him eligible to play any
number of positions. They may have drafted him as a cornerback, but who knew what would happen in training
camp? With those hands and that speed, Delonte could
even join Torrian's wide receivers core.

His muscles relaxed as the tension flowed out of him.
It was amazing what five minutes of clear thinking could
do for the body and mind.

Shoving his cell phone into the pocket of his baggy
sweats, Jared headed back for the media room. On the
way there, he spotted Chyna in the kitchen, leaning
against the refrigerator eating a peach.

"I thought you didn't need anything but me?" Jared
said, sauntering over to her and gliding his palms over
her hips.

"Well, you were taking too long. Besides, I don't think
you have anything that can top this peach. It is divine,"
she said, biting into the fruit's ripe flesh. A droplet of
juice clung to her lip, like an engraved invitation for his
tongue.

"Hmm…" he murmured, wrapping his arms around
her waist and pulling her in direct contact with his hardening body. He lowered his head. "Let's see if I can prove
you wrong."

Chyna brushed her fingers across the soft fabric of Jared's tuxedo as they walked arm in arm to their box seats
at the Metropolitan Opera House at Lincoln Center. She
was having a hard time controlling her emotions. She'd
been to the famed opera house only one time, back when
she was a little girl and Liani's father had surprised them
both with tickets to a performance of *The Nutcracker*.

The sheer opulence was overwhelming enough, but when she thought of all the great performers who had graced this stage…it was enough to make any girl who'd ever had dreams of the doing the same a little emotional.

"Right this way," the usher instructed, his hand gesturing to the closed door of one of the Grand Tier private boxes. How Jared had managed to get these seats was beyond her.

Jared motioned for her to go in ahead of him. Chyna stepped forward and let out a short gasp. There was a small round table with a bottle of champagne chilling in a silver wine bucket. On a platter next to it lay an array of cheeses and fruit, along with a single red rose.

Chyna turned to Jared and grabbed his face between her hands, pulling him to her and crushing her lips to his.

"Thank you," she said. "This is the best present I've ever received."

They took their seats and Jared poured them both glasses of champagne. Chyna's eyes roamed the opera house, trying to see as much as possible before the lights were dimmed at the start of the performance. As she peeked around the privacy partition that partially shielded their box, she noticed something.

"The other boxes on this level have at least six people. How did we get a box for two?" she asked. Jared flashed her a quick, almost guilty look, and comprehension settled in. "You bought out the entire box?" she asked.

Chyna didn't want to even imagine how much one ticket in the nosebleed section cost for a sold-out, one-night-only performance of the Kirov Ballet. An entire box on the Grand Tier level had to have cost a small fortune.

"You better not mention money," Jared said in a

warning tone. He leaned over and placed a kiss on the tip of her nose. "Whatever the cost, it was worth it to have you all to myself." He placed his hands on her shoulders. "Now, I want you to sit down and enjoy the performance."

He turned her around and removed the black shawl from her shoulders. Chyna heard his swift intake of breath and smiled. She'd known exactly what his reaction would be when she'd chosen this particular dress. Jared didn't disappoint.

"You are killing me, woman," he said.

The silky black dress looked perfectly innocent from the front, clinging delicately to her curves and stopping just above her knees. The back told a different story. It dipped incredibly low, leaving her completely bare down to the small of her back.

"I take it you like the dress?"

"Not as much as I'm going to like taking it off you tonight," he answered. "How long is this damn ballet supposed to last?"

"Don't you dare rush this." Chyna laughed. "I want to enjoy every minute of it."

The lights in the opera house blinked several times, indicating that patrons were to take their seats for the start of the performance.

Jared gestured for her to sit as the lights in the opera house dimmed and those facing the stage brightened. He pulled his chair so close that their thighs touched.

He leaned over, and with his warm breath fanning her neck, whispered softly, "I hope this turns out to be the best night of your life."

Chyna looked him in the eyes and said, "It already is."

Jared could think of a million things he'd rather do than sit through a ballet, but he wouldn't trade this night for anything. Watching Chyna as she looked on in complete rapture was worth every penny he'd spent—and damn, had he spent a lot of those to score this box—and every minute he had to endure stuffed in this uncomfortable tuxedo.

She had been captivated from the moment the performers first flitted across the stage, emitting tiny gasps with every twirl of the ballerinas. Jared had no doubt in his mind that her passion for dance rivaled what he felt for football. It was in her blood, in her very soul. He knew the feeling. He was starting to feel it for something else. Chyna.

The realization caused instant panic to grip his chest, but Jared quelled it. He wouldn't allow his fear of being hurt again get in the way of loving another woman, especially one as special at Chyna.

The gold curtains descended as intermission began, and Chyna finally turned her attention away from the stage. The pure joy on her face was inspiring. She looked as if he'd given her the world by bringing her here.

Her chest rose with a deep, contented sigh. "Isn't it just marvelous?"

"The best." Jared nodded as if he'd paid attention to anything happening on the stage. His entire focus had centered on Chyna, relishing her enjoyment.

Chyna proceeded to spend the next ten minutes telling him the story behind the ballet. Jared couldn't care less about Prince Ivan or the magical bird he captured, but Chyna's enthusiasm was infectious.

"I've always loved the story of the Firebird, but never got the chance to see an actual performance of it." She leaned over and kissed him. "Thank you so much for this, Jared. You have no idea how much it means to me."

The excitement she exuded gave him a pretty good

idea. Jared used it to his advantage. Pulling her onto his lap, he settled her bare back to his chest and pressed a kiss onto the fragrant, smooth skin between her shoulder blades.

"You can show me how grateful you are later," he said.

She rubbed her backside against him, snuggling more firmly onto his lap. "That's a promise," she said.

Jared sucked in a swift breath as need raced through him. This ballet couldn't end fast enough.

Mercifully, the lights dimmed. Music poured from the orchestra as the performers returned, and Chyna was once again enraptured. Jared barely registered the dancer floating across the stage. He couldn't concentrate on anything other than the woman in his arms.

His body was a slave to the sensations overwhelming him as Chyna remained in his lap, her firm, round backside nestled against his rapidly hardening shaft. Jared ran his palms along her thighs, sliding his hands underneath the hem of her silky dress.

"Jared," Chyna whispered. "What are you doing?"

He would show her better than he could tell her. Moving quickly to the whisper of lace covering her delectable mound, he hooked a finger around the thin strip of fabric and pushed it to the side. Lifting her slightly with one hand, Jared used the other to free himself from the confines of his tuxedo pants. With one deft, swift move, he shifted her a few inches to the right and entered, impaling her with his rock-hard erection.

"Oh, God," Chyna gasped, her narrow, wet passage clutching around him. For several seconds Jared held her there, letting their bodies get acquainted with their position. Then with even, unhurried strokes, he guided her down his stiff arousal, concentrating on every nuance of her tight, slick body cloaking him as she rose up and down the length of his cock.

He was aware of the people in boxes on either side of them. The thought of being overheard caused a slight thrill to race down his spine. He'd never made love in public before, where there was a chance of getting caught. It made the pleasure even more intense.

With her hands on the brass railing, Chyna pumped up and down, riding him in a deliberate rhythm. Jared pressed his mouth to the small of her back, gliding his tongue up her spine. She grabbed one of his hands and shoved it inside her dress, clamping it onto her breast.

He plucked at her distended nipple, rubbing the hardened point between his thumb and forefinger. With his other hand he snaked around her waist and delved into the soaking wet curls between her legs, finding the rigid nub and giving it the same treatment as her nipple.

Chyna arched her back and swallowed a scream, her body convulsing, shuddering around him as she came apart in his arms. Jared caught her at her waist before she could tip over, peppering her sweat-slicked spine with light kisses.

Her body went limp as she fell back against his chest.

Jared splayed one palm over her stomach while running the other up and down her damp thigh.

"Why haven't I come to the ballet sooner?" he whispered into her ear. "I had no idea what I was missing."

Chapter 13

Chyna stared at the tiny hourglass figure on her computer screen as the huge file continued to download. She tried to remember what she was supposed to do with it once the download was complete, but her focus was on everything *but* work today. She should have taken the day off. It was her birthday, after all. No one would fault her for using a vacation day.

But her wanting time away from the office had nothing to do with celebrating her twenty-seventh birthday. She needed time just to digest all that was happening in her world.

Her advisor had emailed to say he would have word on her independent study project some time this afternoon. Chyna was checking her personal email at a rate of three times per minute, willing an email to pop up.

After six long years, the thought of finally finishing her degree should have had her teetering on the edge of nirvana, but it was the call she'd received an hour ago from the Saberrettes executive director that had caused Chyna's heart to skip several beats before she gained control of it again.

The executive director had praised the work Chyna had done over the past several weeks. Then she'd hit her with the most unexpected, and most incredible news ever. She'd offered her a full-time job as the Saberrettes' permanent choreographer.

Even now Chyna's entire being nearly erupted with excited, nervous energy. To dance for a living had been her dream since the age of six. There was nothing she'd ever wanted more, and she had finally been offered the chance to do just that.

The first person she wanted to tell was Jared, and wasn't that just the most unbelievable thing in all of this?

It was pure madness, the way this man had burrowed himself into every facet of her life. Thoughts of him were constant. It didn't matter if she was in a departmental meeting, helping her mother with her extra laundry work or walking Summer around the block. Thoughts of what Jared was doing, what he was thinking, what sensual games he was planning for their next night together, continued to imbue her brain.

Chyna pulled in a shuddering breath.

She didn't want to admit to it—would ferociously deny it if anyone had the audacity to accuse her. But in her heart she knew she had fallen hopelessly, desperately in love with him. She'd told herself she didn't have time for a man, but Chyna couldn't refute the fact that these past few months with Jared had been some of the most carefree days and pleasure-filled nights of her life.

"Chyna, can I have a word with you in my office?"

She looked up from the computer screen to find her

immediate supervisor, Darla Nash, standing just over her cubicle wall.

"Of course," Chyna answered, pushing away from her desk and following the woman into her sparsely furnished office. Darla motioned for her to take a seat as she walked to the other side of her frosted glass-topped desk and sat behind it. "Richard will be here in a moment. Oh, there he is," she said, as the head of the Risk Assessment division walked in and closed the door behind him.

"Sorry about that," he said, taking the seat opposite Chyna. "The meeting ran a little long. So, did you all discuss the position yet?"

Darla shook her head. "Not yet. My conference call ran over, so we're just getting started."

"Perfect," Richard said with a huge smile.

Chyna looked back and forth between the two, her heart racing like a wild stallion in her chest. "Well, Chyna." Richard Boswell twisted in his chair and clamped his hands together. "As you know, we've been looking for someone to fill one of the junior management positions in the Risk Assessment division. Several members of the team got together last night and decided that you are the best fit for the job."

Chyna had to bite the inside of her cheek to stop herself from screaming.

Omigod. Omigod. Omigod. The litany ran through her mind like a scratched vinyl album stuck on the same verse. She covertly pulled in a calming breath and channeled her inner professional businesswoman.

"Thank you," she said. "Thank you both for having such confidence in me."

"I've no doubt you'll be great," Richard said. "You're going to have your degree in the next few weeks, correct?"

Chyna nodded.

"Excellent," Richard said. "You should know that there will be some changes in the way our junior management team functions here at Marlowe and Brown, and we're going to start instituting them as we transition you into the position."

A measure of unease crept up the back of her neck. "Okay," Chyna said. "Can I ask what kind of changes?"

Darla sat forward in her chair. "We want the junior managers to be cross-functional, so that when they are ready to move into upper management positions, they will have a more well-rounded view of the way the entire organization operates. When you move into your new job, you will be working in both Risk Assessment and Planning. It will seem like a lot in the beginning, but if you focus and perform, you're going to move up the ladder much quicker than people have in the past.

"I've watched you grow over these last few years, Chyna," Darla continued. "I know you're going to excel in this position. If you accept it, of course."

"I appreciate the vote of confidence," Chyna said. She did her best to ignore the apprehension that caused her skin to itch. She shook hands with the division head and then with her immediate supervisor. "You'll understand if I want to take some time to think it over?"

"Absolutely," Darla said. "If you have any questions, you know I'm always here."

"Literally and figuratively," Richard joked.

"One of the hazards of the job," Darla returned with a tired smile.

The lines of fatigue that could not be covered with Darla's makeup sent those ripples of unease skittering across Chyna's skin once again.

As she made her way back to her cubicle, she did

everything within her power to convince herself that she was thrilled at this news. She'd just gotten what she wanted, a stable, well-paying position that would provide financial security. This is what she'd worked for, the end goal of countless nights of studying and days of working her fingers to the bone.

So why did her stomach feel like lead?

It didn't take a lot of soul searching for Chyna to uncover the source of the turmoil roiling through her. For years, she'd had conflicting goals warring with each other. One side wanted nothing more than to prove that her lifelong pursuit of making a living at dancing wasn't just a foolish dream, while another—the sensible, prudent side that could never completely shut out her father's constant proclamation that dreams were worthless—believed she needed a "real" job to succeed in life.

Chyna didn't know what to do. Should she step out on faith and try to make a living from dance or settle for the stability of a normal nine-to-five?

It was an impossible decision. She'd worked hard for both, but there was no way she could feasibly do both. She had to make a choice.

The question was, which was she willing to give up?

Jared tightened the athletic tape around his wrist and tore the piece off with his teeth. Even though the X-ray showed no fracture, the sprained joint still hurt like a bitch. He moved his hand up and down, then rotated it a few times, trying to loosen it up.

A wrist injury was never good for any football player, but for a cornerback it was ten times worse. He used his hands to defend the ball. With only one functioning at full capacity, it made his job that much tougher. Now he had the precarious task of trying to impress the coaches while also making sure he didn't injure himself further before the start of the regular season.

"You ready to roll?" Randall asked, fitting a pair of fingerless gloves on his hands.

Jared nodded, rising from the chair in front of his locker.

"You better put on your best smile. Kendall said there are about a dozen camera crews out there today."

Jared let out a frustrated curse. "Why do they let the press into OTAs? It's not as if this is training camp. Some of the guys are just getting back from vacation today. Now all you're going to hear about is how rusty everyone looked during the organized team activities."

"They won't be able to say that about the two of us," Randall said. "Maybe more of the guys will spend their off season in the gym instead of scoping out the buffet on a cruise boat."

"After the way Cedric came back smiling, I may take a cruise around the Caribbean myself," Jared said. "Though I think it has more to do with who he brought with him instead of the location."

"I would be smiling if I had a woman like Payton Mosely on my arm, too," Randall agreed.

Jared didn't have to covet Cedric's woman. He had his own, and she was every bit as fine as any woman he'd ever seen.

A grin flashed across his lips at the thought of the birthday dinner he had planned for Chyna tonight. He'd made reservations at Masa, one of the hottest and most exclusive Japanese restaurants in Manhattan. His real estate agent had delivered the deed to the dance school this morning, just before he'd headed to the Sabers compound. His housekeeper, Maggie, was having the deed gift-wrapped.

In the field house, the bulk of the Sabers' defense was congregating around the forty-five-yard line on the practice field. The team was still in noncontact mode, so players wouldn't be required to dress in full pads for another couple of weeks, but some of the guys still opted for their practice jerseys instead of T-shirts as they walked through the plays. Jared understood the psychology behind it. He always felt more in work mode when wearing a jersey.

As he and Randall approached, a couple of the guys who were huddled around each other broke apart and cast cautious looks toward them.

"What?" Jared asked, his tone brooking no tolerance for bull. If they had heard something regarding his position, he wanted to know now.

Starting tight end Kendall Fisher lifted his iPhone. "You don't happen to keep tabs on some of the guys on Twitter, do you?" he asked.

"I don't do Twitter," Jared said.

"Yeah, well…Carlos Garcia just posted that he and Samantha are engaged," Kendall said.

Shock siphoned the thoughts from Jared's brain. He didn't know what to think, was unsure of how he should even feel. A part of him didn't want to care. He was done with Samantha, had finally expunged her from his heart. It shouldn't matter to him what she did.

Yet an even bigger part was mad as hell. He'd dropped hints about marriage more than once while they were together, but she had never been ready. In his last attempt he'd shelled out over thirty thousand dollars for an engagement ring and had been ready to promise her a lifetime of happiness as his wife. And now, just months after they start dating, she was marrying Carlos Garcia?

Cold rage settled into Jared's bones, turning his blood to ice.

For ten years Samantha had done nothing but take. And he'd been all too happy to give. As usual.

He'd spent his entire life taking care of other people, whether it was silently holding his mother's hand while she cried herself to sleep when his father left to be with his other women or providing capital when one of his friends needed extra money to help fund his dream. It was what he did. He didn't know how else to be.

The one thing he had never regretted was asking the shy, beautiful college sophomore out to dinner. And then, when he'd found out that she'd grown up stricken by poverty, he'd jumped at the chance to give her everything her heart desired.

Jared regretted it now. He wished he had walked right past Samantha Miller that day he'd spotted her sitting on a bench outside Hepner Hall back on campus at San Diego State.

Randall nudged his shoulder. "Hey, man, don't even sweat it. You're better off without her."

"You're damned right about that," Jared said through clenched teeth.

But as he went through the first set of drills with the rest of the Sabers' defensive secondary unit, Jared couldn't get his mind off Samantha and how blind he had been to her lying, treacherous ways. He missed two easy interceptions, and got beat by the wide receiver more times than he could count.

"Dawson," Lyle Cross, the Sabers' defensive coordinator, barked. "I cut you some slack on the interceptions because of the wrist, but you give me one good damn reason why I shouldn't light into your ass for missing that tackle? This team is not getting shut out of the playoffs because you can't get past the guy blocking you."

"I'm sorry," Jared said. "I've just… I've got a lot on my mind."

"I don't give a damn about what's on your mind," Cross bellowed, his hot breath blasting Jared in the face. "The only thing that should be on your mind right now is sticking to that wide receiver's ass and making sure he doesn't catch the damn ball. You got that?"

"Yes," Jared answered.

It took every ounce of willpower he had to remain on that field, when all he wanted to do was go in the shower and let the hot spray beat down on him. The rest of the secondary core was quiet as everyone calmly got back into position and ran through the play again.

They rotated positions, changing out the first string for the second. To Jared's infinite disgust, the newly drafted rookie, Delonte Cannon, defended the ball like a seasoned veteran. Jared stood on the sideline, hands on his hips, looking on in frustration.

"What's up with you, man?" Randall demanded. "You need to get your head in the game. In case you hadn't noticed, that rookie is gunning for your job. And the way you're playing right now, it looks as if you're trying to give it to him."

Jared stared at the players on the field without really seeing them. His mind was still reeling from the news about Samantha. He had a hard time concentrating on anything else.

How long had she been playing him? She and Carlos had to have been seeing each other for months, maybe even years, for the two of them to get engaged so soon. She'd been messing around on him behind his back—that was the only explanation. After everything he'd done for her.

"Jared!" Randall barked.

He looked over at his teammate. "What?"

"First string is backup." Randall motioned to the field.

As they sprinted toward players congregating at the twenty-five yard line, Randall caught his arm and slowed down their run. "This is no joke, Jared. You can lose your starting position if you don't show up in this next series. You'd better put Sam and Carlos and Chyna and everything else out of your mind right now, because if you don't, that rookie is going to take your spot."

Jared nodded, knowing he should take Randall's warning to heart. He was on the verge of hobbling his career. Samantha had already taken so much from him. He wouldn't give her the power to ruin football for him, too.

But as Jared went through the next succession of plays, he couldn't keep his head in the game. He continued to falter, getting chewed out by the coach a second time, then pulled out of the first string rotation.

As he watched the rookie cornerback move into his spot, Jared told himself this was just a temporary setback. Once he got his head on straight, everything would return to normal and he would be back in the starting lineup when the Sabers opened their preseason game in another month.

But when Delonte Cannon made a spectacular one-handed interception, a boulder settled in the pit of Jared's stomach. He had a sinking feeling his fate had been sealed.

Chyna stood before the door to one of three conditioning rooms at the Sabers' practice compound. Now

that organized team activities had started and the players required full use of the field, the dance squad was
regulated to this smaller room.

For the fourth time in the last five minutes, Chyna
gripped the door's steel handle then let it go. She bit her
bottom lip, trying to stop the quivering that had started
the minute she walked out the doors of Marlowe and
Brown. If she didn't get her emotions under control now
there was no way she would be able to halt the tears that
had been on the brink of falling since she'd made the decision to turn down the Saberrettes' job offer.

She had run every scenario she could think of through
her mind, but no matter how she tried to shuffle the
hours, there were still only twenty-four of them in a day.
Not to mention the pay gap. Her new salary at Marlowe
and Brown was nearly twice what the Saberrettes had
offered. But that higher salary came at a steep price.
After her second meeting with Darla, where her supervisor had gone into more detail about the new position,
Chyna learned her workload was about to double.

She'd spent a solid hour deliberating, and had come
to the only viable answer. She couldn't afford not to take
the junior management position.

She had responsibilities that would always be a constant in her life. Taking care of Summer and her parents
were important, but providing for her own financial well-
being had always been at the top of the list. Her new promotion would take care of that.

But what about the two new gifts she had received this
summer? Both the Saberrettes and Jared had claimed a
piece of her heart.

When Chyna weighed all her options, the only expendable thing was the Saberrettes. Even if she could
get the executive director to agree to let her continue as

a part-time freelance choreographer, she was still looking at hours of practices, possibly having to attend road games, and just flat-out exhaustion from the physical exertion. She could no longer afford to commit herself to it, especially if she still wanted to make time for Jared. When comparing the two, it had taken less than a second for Chyna to decide that Jared was more important.

Despite the swiftness in which she'd made her choice, the reality of what she was giving up still showered her in misery. Now that the dance school was possibly closing if they could not find a new owner, every outlet for dance she had would be gone.

Chyna swallowed back the sob that nearly escaped.

As she reached for the door handle, the door opened.

Liani, who was on the other side, jumped back in surprise. "Hey there! It's about time, birthday girl. I've been calling you all day."

"I'm sorry. My cell phone has been on vibrate since this morning. I guess I didn't feel it," Chyna said, then she gave herself away with a sniff and hiccup. She was definitely going to bawl her eyes out before she left the facility today.

"What's the matter?" Liani asked, instant worry creasing her forehead. "Oh, my God, is it your dad? Is he okay?"

"Yeah, yeah." Chyna waved off her concern. "He's fine."

"So what's going on? Something's bothering you. Oh, wait. Is it Jared? Did he go crazy on you after hearing that crap about his ex-girlfriend?"

"No. What about his ex?" Chyna asked with another sniff.

"She and Carlos Garcia are getting married. You didn't hear?"

Chyna shook her head. She wondered if Jared had tried to call her phone. "I haven't talked to him all day," she told Liani.

"Then what's up with you? You're scaring me."

"I'm sorry. I didn't mean to. It's good news, actually," Chyna said with a sad smile. "I got the promotion."

Liani's eyes ballooned. "Oh, my God. Congratulations! That's awesome."

She wrapped her arms around Chyna and squeezed. Liani stepped back, but held on to her hands. "So what's with the doom and gloom?" But before Chyna could answer, realization dawned in her friend's eyes. "Oh, no. You'll have to quit on us, won't you?"

Chyna's lip quivered as she nodded.

Liani's shoulders slumped. "I had a feeling this would happen from the minute you told me you were being considered. Oh, honey, I'm sorry. I know how much this job with the Saberrettes has meant to you." She gave Chyna another hug. "You have to do what you have to do. Sucks being a grown-up, doesn't it?"

Chyna nodded again. "It does."

"Let's go tell the rest of the squad," Liani said, rubbing her hand up and down Chyna's arm. "Tonight, we have margaritas. And you do not get to back out on me."

"It's a deal," Chyna said with a tearful laugh.

They entered the room and walked to where the squad was practicing. The newer girls still looked nervous, congregating amongst themselves.

"Hi, ladies," Chyna started. "I've got some news." She looked over the faces of the women she'd become friends with over the past two months, hating what she was about to say. "I can no longer work as the Saberrettes' choreographer."

A flurry of *whats, no ways* and *whys* flitted around the room.

"I hate to do this, but I just accepted a new position at my day job, and it's going to take more time than I first realized."

"Yeah, right," came a sarcastic reply. Chyna turned to find Kenya Simmons standing just to the right of her, a hand on her hip and a cynical grimace scrunching up her face. "Just because they call you 'The Brain' doesn't mean you are the only person with one, Chyna. We are not stupid," Kenya spat. "We can see what's going on."

"I just told you what's going on," Chyna said.

"Everybody here has jobs outside of the squad, except for trust fund babies like that one." She gestured to Liani.

"Hey," Liani said, taking a step forward.

Chyna put a hand to her friend's chest, holding her back. "My new position will require me to work at least ten hours a day," Chyna said, upset that she had to explain herself.

"Cut the bull," Kenya snarled. "This new job isn't the reason you're quitting. You no longer have to be the Saberrettes' choreographer because you've already got what you wanted. Jared Dawson."

"What?"

"Oh, sure, you came here with your little song about how much dancing means to you, yet as soon as you land yourself a fine, rich Sabers player, you're out the door. That's no coincidence."

"Jared has nothing to do with my decision to leave," Chyna protested.

Kenya raised her hands up. "I'm not mad at you, honey. If you can get yourself a Saber, more power to you, but don't look down your nose at the rest of us. Because, guess what, Chyna? You are just like the girls on this squad who are trying to make the most of this situation. Except you don't have to follow the same rules we do. You get to have Jared and no one bats an eye." Kenya slapped her palms together with three very pronounced claps, "Bravo." With pure venom in her glare, she pivoted and started for the other side of the room.

Several members of the squad came over and gave her hugs, but Chyna hardly registered their goodbyes and wishes of good luck. She wanted to snatch Kenya by her weave and tear her eyes out.

Chyna's throat clogged with anger. Taking the job with the Saberrettes had *never* been about landing a man for her. She'd agreed to work as the squad's choreographer because she loved to dance. Period.

"Don't let her get to you," Liani said, throwing a comforting arm over Chyna's shoulders. "She's just jealous because none of the dozen players she's slept with will give her the time of day once they're through with her."

"It doesn't matter why she said it," Chyna argued. "What matters is that everyone is going to think it's true. They probably already do."

"Who cares what the rest of them think?" Liani said. "If they weren't jealous of your relationship with Jared they would be jealous because of your height, or your boobs or whatever else intimidates them."

Liani gripped her arm and turned her around to face her. Staring into her eyes, she said, "Forget them, Chyna. What you've found with Jared is rare and it's real. Don't let anyone take it away from you. Believe me, something that special is hard to find. When you do, hold on to it.

"I need to get back to practice," Liani said, "And you need to find Jared. After the news about his ex's engagement, he probably needs to be reminded that he's got something even better in you."

"You're right," Chyna said with a firm nod as she hugged her friend.

Liani pointed a finger at her. "So tonight? Margaritas?"

"Yes."

"Unless you're too occupied trying to soothe Jared's ego, of course. I don't want to come between you getting some."

Chyna gave Liani a playful shove. "Get out of here."

"No matter what, you call me tonight, okay, hon?"

"I will," she said, and with one last, shaky breath, she stared at the dance squad members practicing the routine she and Liani had put together.

Chyna couldn't swallow past the lump in her throat as the enormity of what she'd just given up hit her like a blow to the chest. Working with the Saberrettes had fulfilled her lifelong dream of making money through dance. After years of hearing her father harp on how pursing her dream would never amount to anything, she'd finally proven him wrong.

And she'd just given it all up.

Pulling her bottom lip between her teeth to suppress the quivering, Chyna turned her back on the dance squad and walked out of the room.

Chyna made her way through the maze of hallways in the compound, heading to the team's indoor field house where the Sabers' organized team activities were being held. As she rounded a corner, she nearly walked right into Randall Robinson.

"Oh, I'm sorry," she side, sidestepping him.

"Hey, where are you going?" he asked, halting her with a tug on her arm.

"To the practice field. I know you guys are busy, but I was hoping to speak to Jared for a few minutes," she said.

"Don't, okay?" Randall used the hem of his gray Sabers T-shirt, which was mostly darkened with sweat, to wipe his face. "Look, Chyna. Jared is not in a good place right now. This crap with Sam and Carlos has his head all messed up."

"I heard about it. That's one of the reasons I wanted to speak to him."

"He doesn't need anyone bringing it up. Jared needs to concentrate on his game. He's been playing like crap all day, and you going in there and reminding him about Sam isn't going to help. He doesn't need you bothering him right now."

Bothering him?

"That's not for you to decide," Chyna said, getting more irritated by the second. "If Jared doesn't want me around, let *him* tell me."

"Dammit, didn't you hear what I just said?" Randall bit out. "Jared needs to focus on work, and he can't do that with you clinging all over him. You're turning out to be more of a distraction than you were supposed to be." He blew out a curse. "I'm starting to regret suggesting he even bother with one of the Saberrettes."

Chyna's spine stiffened. "What did you say?" she asked in an icy whisper.

"I said to leave him alone." Randall's warning tone escalated her ire even more. "You did your job, okay. You got his mind off Samantha and showed him a good time during the off-season, but now that OTAs have started you need to back off. Jared can't handle any more distractions if he's going to keep his starting position."

Randall turned and headed back toward the field house.

As she stared at his retreating back, Chyna could hardly see past the hurt that seized her entire being as her world began to crumble around her.

Chapter 14

Jared adjusted the temperature on the rapid wine chiller and checked the digital readout on his stove. He expected the building concierge to announce Chyna's arrival any minute.

He grabbed two crystal goblets from the cabinet and set them next to the silver tray of fruit and cheese Maggie had laid out before she left twenty minutes ago. A thin, rectangular box with crisp dark brown paper and an elaborate blue, brown and cream bow sat a few inches away, along with a dozen white roses and a cupcake with fancy sprinkles and a single birthday candle.

He'd debated greeting Chyna at the door with the box that held the deed to the dance school, but that wasn't part of tonight's plan. In his head he'd envisioned how the evening would pan out. He'd welcome Chyna with a kiss and guide her to the kitchen for a glass of wine and her birthday cupcake. He'd let her see the box and speculate on what was inside, but he wouldn't let her open it. Not until after they were done with dinner at Masa, where she would cut into the birthday cake he was having delivered to the restaurant for dessert. He'd sent the key to the dance school to be baked inside of it.

He would then hand over the box with the deed, and they would come back here where he'd get the hot sex he'd been thinking about for hours.

If anyone could help him get his mind off the catastrophe this day had been, it was Chyna. To hell with Samantha and Carlos and their wedding. More than anything, Jared was pissed at himself for allowing the news to affect him at all. Samantha Miller didn't matter to him anymore.

He had Chyna. She was all he needed.

The buzzer sounded and the concierge announced that Miss Chyna McCrea was on her way up. Jared grabbed the cellophane-wrapped flowers from the shelf and hurried to the door. A few moments later there was a soft knock. He opened the door and couldn't stop himself from going straight for her lips.

"Happy birthday, baby," he said against her mouth. Jared felt her stiffen. He took a step back and peered at her. "Are you okay?" he asked.

She didn't answer, just wrapped her arms around her middle and walked into the foyer.

Alarm tightening his chest, Jared placed the flowers on the table next to the door and walked over to where Chyna stood just inside the arched entryway to his kitchen. He stepped up behind her and captured her upper arms in his hands.

"Baby, what's going on?"

She shook free of his hold and swung around, her eyes teeming with anger.

"Has this all been some joke to you?" she asked in a raw, hoarse whisper.

Jared's head snapped back. "What?"

"This thing between us? Was it just a game, something for you to do over the summer that you could go back and tell all of your little football friends about when the new season starts up?"

"Chyna, where the hell is this coming from? No, this isn't just some game. Why would you even ask me that?"

"Oh, so are you saying I'm *not* just a distraction? You didn't start seeing me just because you needed something to help get your mind off of your ex-girlfriend?"

Jared's eyelids slid shut.

"You bastard," she bit out.

"Chyna, let me explain."

He reached for her, but she slapped his hand away and sidestepped him. "Don't you dare touch me," she spat as she stormed for the door.

Jared bolted after her. No way was he letting her walk away. Not without talking this out first.

"Chyna, please." He captured her arm. "Give me a chance to explain."

She whipped around and glared at him. The anger and hurt in those soulful gray eyes tore at his heart. Jared ignored the cold knot that had formed in his stomach. They could talk through this. "Can we go into the living room and sit down. Maybe have a glass of wine and discuss this like two rational people?"

"I'm not here to drink wine with you, and I'll be honest, Jared, I'm not feeling all that rational right now. You see, finding out that I'm being used makes me a little crazy."

"I haven't been using you."

"Oh, you know the funniest part in all of this?" she

continued as if he hadn't spoken. "Kenya Simmons was supposed to make the Gatorade run that day. She wouldn't have had a problem being used like a piece of trash, as long as it was one of the Sabers doing the using. It's just your luck that I happened to offer to get the Gatorade instead."

"Chyna, please," Jared pleaded. She was killing him with every word that came out of her mouth. "That's not how it was. You've got to believe me."

"Why should I?"

"If you would just let me explain—"

"Go ahead," she said, the command draped in bitterness. "But you've got two minutes. After that, I'm out of here."

"Dammit," Jared cursed. "Okay. Fine." He rubbed a hand down his face, trying to figure out the best way to handle this. "At first, yes, you were only supposed to be a distraction." Her head jerked back as if he'd slapped her, and the instant pain that washed over her face clutched at Jared's chest. "But that was before I even talked to you, Chyna. I swear, everything about the time we've spent together has been real. I've—"

He stopped, afraid to lay his feelings bare so soon after having them trampled on. But he couldn't deny the way he felt about her, and more than ever, he needed Chyna to know.

"I've fallen in love with you," he said.

She looked up at him, her eyes luminous and brimming with unshed tears. "How can I believe that?" she whispered. "You've been lying to me from the very beginning."

"It hasn't been a lie," Jared snapped.

She shook her head and huffed out a humorless laugh. "Before I took that job I told myself not to get mixed up with one of you ball players. I'd heard the horror stories, yet I still fell for it. How could I have been this stupid?"

"Dammit, Chyna." Jared stalked to the kitchen and snatched the wrapped box from the counter. He returned to find her still standing in the foyer with her arms crossed stonily across her chest. The tears that had been welling in her eyes had begun to cascade down her smooth cheeks.

"Here," he said, shoving the box toward her. She looked down at it, but her arms remained stubbornly crossed. "Would you take it?" Jared urged.

"What is it?" she asked, cautiously, angrily.

"It's supposed to be your birthday present," he bit out. "I sure as hell hadn't pictured giving it to you like this, but since you're having such a hard time believing how I feel about you, maybe this will show you."

As if it were a snake lying in wait, she inched her hand toward the box and gently plucked it from his fingers. She lifted the top and drew the tri-folded sheaf of papers. Jared studied her face as she unfolded the papers and trailed her eyes down the deed.

When she looked up at him, the gratitude he'd been expecting was nowhere to be found. Instead, her stare was more venomous than ever.

"You don't get it at all, do you?" she asked.

"Apparently not," he said. "I just gave you a damn dance studio, and you look as if you're ready to tear my head off."

"Did I *ask* you for this damn dance studio?" she shouted. She threw her hands in the air. "God, Jared, you *just don't get it.* Do you know how long I've had to fend for myself? All my life. If I wanted something, I couldn't rely on anyone else to get it."

"What does that have to do with this, Chyna?"

Her eyes flashed with fiery outrage. She strutted up to him, her jaw pure stone. In a deadly quiet voice, she said, "I told you from the very beginning that I didn't need you to take care of me. The only way I want to own this school is if I can find a way to buy it myself. I don't want it to be handed to me as if its payment for services rendered."

"That is not what this is," Jared said. God, how had this become so messed up? "The school is supposed to be a *gift,* Chyna. I know how much you wanted it."

"So you dip into your rainy day fund and pull out a couple of hundred grand, right? No big deal."

Jared shook his head, unsure of what else he could say to make her see reason.

"I don't need you stepping in and saving the day, Jared. In fact, I don't need you at all."

She turned, and with a cold calm, headed for the door. She placed the box with the deed on the table next to the roses, and quietly closed the door behind her.

Curled up in a blanket on her futon, Chyna tightened her hold on Summer as she wiped at the tears that continued to track down her face. Her cell phone started humming again, shimmying across her coffee table. She leaned over and checked the caller ID, letting it go to voice mail when she saw Liani's number.

Eventually, her friend would get the idea and stop calling. Either that, or the voice mail would fill up. Between Liani and Jared, there were over twenty messages clogging her voice mail system.

Her house phone rang. After a few moments the answering machine picked up.

"Chyna, I've tried calling your cell phone, but I guess Jared has you too occupied to answer," came Liani's voice. "You never showed up for drinks this evening. Give me a call when you get home."

Chyna thought about calling her friend back, but waved off the thought. She didn't have the energy to do any more than what she was doing right now, clinging to a five-pound dog for support and crying like a school-girl who'd just been dumped by her first crush. Only *she* had been the one to do the dumping, and now it was up to her to convince herself she'd done the right thing.

She'd known what she was getting herself into—Liani had shared too many tales of brokenhearted Saberrettes for Chyna to plead ignorance. Yet, she'd fallen for it anyway.

Jared had used her.

Even if his feelings had changed over the course of their time together, to know that the only reason he'd first asked her out was to get his mind off his ex-girlfriend was the worst kind of blow to her tender ego. She'd been expendable; just one in a sea of interchangeable women at his disposal.

What if she'd turned down his dinner invitation the day he'd sought her out at the Patisserie? Would he have tried again, or did he operate on a three-strikes-and-you're-out basis? Would he have just moved on to another member of the Saberrette squad and spent the summer making love to Kenya, or Jamie or one of the other girls?

The thought sent a rod of pain so deep, so fierce, it sliced straight through her chest and into her heart.

She had to get past this. She couldn't allow thoughts of what she could have had with Jared to consume her any more than they already had.

Despite his motives for being with her, Chyna was forced to concede that Jared had taught her a valuable lesson. He'd taught her the importance of enjoying life. She could not deny the joy she'd experienced this summer. She may never know what the time they shared had meant to him, but for her, it had been real. She would cherish it for what it was, but now, it was time to move on.

Chyna pushed herself up from the spot she'd occupied for the past four hours. With determination and stubborn pride spurring her on, she barreled full steam ahead with her effort to push Jared Dawson out of her life.

Chapter 15

His arms folded across his chest, Jared tilted the chair back until it hit the edge of the table behind him. Secluded in the darkened film room, he studied the video from yesterday's practice with single-minded focus, determined to correct every misstep he'd made on the field. He had a hard time spotting any.

For the past two weeks, every ounce of his concentration had been on the game. He ate, slept and breathed football, pouring over playbooks and notes back from his college days, and studying every frame of film from every single professional game he'd ever played.

He was the first player to make it to the field house in the morning, running sprints, lifting weights, doing his damnedest to block out everything but the game. His only goal was making sure he remained the starting cornerback for the New York Sabers.

It was time he started taking care of his damned self. He'd spent his entire life going to bat for everyone else, and where the hell had it gotten him? Right where he was, sitting in a dark room alone, with nothing but his skills on the football field to count on.

Jared sucked in a deep, shuddering breath, willing his mind to focus on the projector screen. He wouldn't think about the special boot camp taking place for the five newest rookies on the Sabers squad, and how during yesterday's drills, Delonte Cannon had finally cracked under the pressure. He didn't want to retain his starting position because of someone else's mistakes. He wanted to keep it because he was the best man for the job.

He wouldn't think about the magazine cover he'd spotted at a newsstand this morning with a picture of Samantha flashing a rock the size of a golf ball. He was done with that. Finally, *irrevocably* done.

His newfound armor of resolve would be impenetrable if not for the one person who continued to invade his mind. No matter how hard he tried, Jared could not shake the memory of the last time he'd seen Chyna. Visions of the pain that had clouded her face when she'd asked if she had only been a distraction for him. The virulence in her eyes when he gave her the deed to the dance school.

Buying the school had been a bad move. He realized that now. For the past two weeks the argument had played back and forth in his mind, and Jared had finally started to see things from her perspective.

Chyna wasn't the type of woman who sat back and waited for someone to come to her rescue. She was strong, independent. He hadn't considered how she would see the gift he'd purchased for her, but if he'd taken the time to think about it, he could have anticipated that she'd react exactly as she had.

That self-reliant streak of hers was one of the things that he'd had the hardest time accepting in the beginning of their relationship, yet it was the thing he'd come to respect most about her. So why in the hell had he thought she'd fall into his arms with gratitude when he'd handed her the deed to that school?

Jared ran a hand down his face, throwing his head back with a harsh sigh.

He knew why he'd assumed she'd be overwhelmed with appreciation, but the answer was too harsh to face, the truth too pathetic to swallow. He'd expected it because it's what he needed her to do in order to make *him* feel worthwhile.

Looking at himself with an ice-cold eye, Jared questioned his motivation for every good deed he'd done over these last few years. The reflection that mirror presented weighed in his stomach like an anvil. He was always so damned concerned with playing the part of the hero—the one who could be counted on to take care of everyone else—that it had started to define him. It's why he'd stayed with Samantha for so long. She'd fed his desire to be the caregiver.

But he didn't have to be that person with Chyna. Chyna wanted him for *him,* not for what he could provide for her.

He had to get her back. It couldn't be too late.

Jared powered down the projector system, knocking over his chair in his haste to leave. He walked out of the film room and found Randall leaning against the wall on the other side of the hallway, arms crossed and a frown furrowing his brow. Jared paused at the sight of his teammate, then started for the exit doors.

"So you gonna just keep ignoring me?" Randall called after him.

"Damn right," Jared said. He would have continued down the corridor, but Randall caught his elbow, halting his forward motion. Jared jerked his arm away. "I'm warning you, Randall. Stay the hell away from me."

"Man, I told you I was sorry. I never would have said anything to her if I had known it was that serious between the two of you."

"You shouldn't have said anything. Period," Jared bit out. "Just because you jump from one bed to another, it doesn't mean that's how everyone else wants to live their life." He took a menacing step forward, pointing a finger at Randall's chest. "From now on, stay the hell out of my business."

He pushed past his teammate and stalked out of the building. Jared continued to seethe as he stormed across the parking lot toward his car.

"Jared! Wait up!" he heard Torrian's voice call.

He continued walking, pretending he hadn't heard him, but his friend caught up to him before Jared reached his car.

Jared swore under his breath. "Whatever it is will have to wait, Wood. I've got something I need to do."

"Yeah, like get your ass back in there." Torrian blew out a ragged breath. "Your phone's about to ring with a call from Tom Rutledge."

The Sabers' general manager? What the hell?

"If this is about my performance when camp first started, I would think I've made up for it these past two weeks," Jared said.

Torrian was shaking his head. "It's not about that." He paused. "They know about you being at the Rio in Atlantic City on Super Bowl Sunday. It's proof that you violated your agreement with the team."

Chyna watched the time in the bottom right-hand corner of her computer screen click from 8:58 to 8:59 p.m. She'd vowed two hours ago that she would not put in another fourteen-hour workday, but unless a fairy god-mother floated from the sky and magically completed the report that was due tomorrow, her vow would be broken for the third night in a row. Twenty minutes later, Chyna emailed the report to her supervisor and turned the lights off in her starkly furnished office.

She'd often wondered why Darla's office was so bare. She now realized that the woman most likely couldn't find a spare minute to decorate. Chyna grimaced at the plant she'd brought for her desk the day she moved into her new office. The leaves were curling in on themselves and browning at the edges, but she was too tired to worry about watering it.

She locked up her office and moved sluggishly down the quiet corridor. Just the thought of being back here in a little over eight hours made her want to throw up her dinner…if she'd had the time to eat dinner.

If there was one silver lining to this storm cloud that had become her life, it was that the subway trains wouldn't be as crowded as they were during evening rush hour. She made it to Bay Ridge just before ten o'clock. She thought about stopping in at the deli a block away from the train station, but waved off the idea. She had cereal at home. Hopefully, the milk wasn't spoiled.

Chyna walked up to her building and stopped cold. Liani was sitting on the stoop, reclining on her elbows as if she belonged there. Her friend nodded to the brief-case Chyna held.

"So, this is how you're spending your time these days?" she asked.

Ignoring the sarcasm, Chyna asked, "How long have you been here?"

Liani shrugged. "I came around eight-thirty. I figured that would give you enough time to wind down from your workday, but wasn't so late to where you'd have already gone to bed. Guess I was off by a few hours."

"I'm sorry. This new job is kicking my butt," Chyna said, climbing the stairs and unlocking the front door to her building.

"You don't have to tell me that. It's written all over your face," Liani commented, falling in step with her as she marched up to her apartment. "How much sleep are you getting?"

"Don't ask," Chyna muttered.

She opened the door and was greeted by an overly excited Summer who pranced around as if she were walking on hot coals. Chyna tossed her briefcase on the coffee table and collapsed onto the futon. Looking over at Liani, who'd stopped just inside the door, she said, "I'm sorry I haven't had a chance to return your calls."

The apology was way overdue. At first, Chyna had been too overwrought to discuss the Jared situation with Liani, but it soon became a matter of not having enough time in the day to breathe. Her new position at Marlowe and Brown consumed her every waking moment.

Summer leaped onto her lap and yipped, her tiny rear end wiggling.

"I think that dog needs to go out," Liani said.

"I've asked her to go on the floor. It's easier to just clean up after her than to walk down three flights, around the block and back up again."

Chyna pushed up from the futon with a groan and grabbed Summer's leash from where it hung on a nail next to the door. The three of them trekked down the stairs and started on a casual stroll around the block.

"So?" Chyna asked. "Is this our girl's night out?"

"Not exactly," Liani said. "I'm here to plead on behalf of someone else."

Chyna glanced over at her, not liking the vibe she was getting from her friend. Then realization dawned. "If Jared sent you here, you can just go."

"He didn't. Randall did."

"Oh." Chyna let out a hollow laugh. "Believe me, mentioning *that* name won't help your case, either. Do you know he's been calling my job? No matter how many times I ask the receptionist not to put his call through, she still does. It's as if it's impossible to say no to Randall Robinson."

"He's kind of hard to resist," Liani mumbled.

"What are you talking about?" Chyna asked.

"Look, Chyna, the fact that Randall even approached me is so much bigger than you can possibly realize. He and I have this unspoken agreement never to interact with each other in any way, shape or form. Not since last season…when…" Liani didn't continue, just regarded her with an uneasy glance before staring at something on the sidewalk.

The truth hit Chyna like a sledgehammer. "You mean it was *him? Randall Robinson* is the Saber you slept with?" Chyna screeched.

"Should I just put it on the JumboTron in Times Square?" Liani said in a terse whisper, glancing at the people they'd just passed sitting on another building's stoop.

"Sorry," Chyna apologized. "He just doesn't seem like your type."

"He's not," Liani protested. "It was one enormous, gigantic, *humongous* mistake. For both of us."

Chyna regarded her friend, her curiosity getting the best of her. "What happened that weekend, Liani? You never told me."

"It's not important."

"Yes, it is. You haven't been the same since." Chyna reached over and took her friend's hand, giving it a concerned squeeze. "Talk to me."

Liani sucked in a deep breath and expelled it with a weary sigh. "It was the night before the Sabers played the San Francisco 49ers," she started. "I wasn't even scheduled to travel with the Saberrettes for that game, but one of the girls got sick. Randall found me in the hotel bar that night. I'd just gotten off the phone with my mom, so you can imagine where my head was at the time."

Chyna had an idea. Liani's relationship with her mother gave new meaning to the word *complicated*.

"I guess he noticed that I was upset. We started talking, and one thing led to another. The next thing I knew, I was waking up in his hotel bed the following morning."

Chyna's head reared back in surprise. "Wow," she said, a bit stunned. "This just seems so out of character. You don't do indiscriminate sex."

"I know. That's why I told him to just forget it ever happened."

"Why would you do that?"

"Because," she said, as if that was answer enough. Chyna motioned for her to continue. "What?" Liani choked out. "Are you kidding me? Randall and I are so incredibly different. It's crazy to even think of us together."

"It cannot be that crazy," Chyna opined. "There must have been something there, some spark of attraction between you two. If there wasn't, you never would have slept with him in the first place."

"It was a mistake," Liani insisted. "Randall and I both agreed that it was just one huge mistake."

"Did he agree, or did you make the choice for the

both of you?" Chyna asked, thinking that her friend was protesting a bit too much for someone who didn't care.

Liani shot her an irritated look. "Randall and I are… we're not even on each other's radar screens, so the fact that he came to me should give you an indication of how serious this is. It's killing him that he's caused so much strife for you and Jared. He said the whole distraction thing was his idea, and that Jared was *never* comfortable with it. He even admitted that he told Jared to go for someone else when you first turned him down, but Jared wouldn't."

Chyna paused. "Randall said that?"

"Yes, the jerk." Liani shook her head. "You know, you are *so* right. He is totally not my type. Who in their right mind would want to be with an arrogant man whore? I mean, he—"

"Hello," Chyna said, cutting her off. "We're back to talking about me now, remember?"

"Oh, yeah. Sorry," Liani said. "So, are you going to talk to Jared? Apparently, he has completely shut himself off from the rest of the team since the two of you broke up."

"I don't know," Chyna said, her heart constricting at the thought of him being miserable. But it started pumping like an oil well at the thought of contacting him.

She wanted to. *God,* did she want to. She went to bed craving the sound of his voice, the touch of his hands upon her skin. She missed him so much.

Liani reached over and gripped her hands. "You really need to, honey. I have never seen you happier than you were this summer. And, I have to tell you, right now, you look like crap."

"Thanks a lot," Chyna groused.

"I'm being honest here. You may look like a million

bucks with your snazzy business suit and those absolutely fierce heels that I am so going to borrow." Liani captured her chin in her fingers. "But from the neck up, I've never seen you so sad. And it breaks my heart. You need to take a serious look at yourself and figure out what it's going to take to make you happy, Chyna. From what I see, you haven't found it."

Liani leaned in to give her a comforting kiss on the cheek and left her standing in the middle of the sidewalk with a dozen questions swirling in her head.

Chapter 16

Jared's eyes roamed the spacious office, taking in the various plaques and trophies on the walls and shelves. Despite not making it to the Super Bowl, Tom Rutledge had been awarded General Manager of the Year for the past two years in a row. It was a well-deserved honor. Rutledge had worked hard to put together a solid team. Every analyst proclaimed the Sabers were on the precipice of something special. As long as they continued to play well and steer clear of off-the-field drama that could affect the team's morale, the Sabers were destined for greatness.

As he sat in the quiet of the GM's office, the storm that had begun brewing in Jared's gut yesterday when Torrian had caught up to him in the parking lot had whipped up to gale force. The twenty-four-hour reprieve he'd received when Rutledge was called away for an emergency meeting with a group of other GMs hadn't done much good for Jared's nerves. He'd spent the entire day stressing about what would happen in today's meeting.

He didn't know what he would do if upper management took the hard nose route and released him from his contract for violation of the no-gambling agreement he'd signed.

The door opened and Jared whipped around.

"Sorry about that," Rutledge said, moving with his signature brisk stride and settling into the chair behind his desk. "This dispute with the player's union is keeping me up at night."

"You don't think they're going to force a lockout, do you?"

"You tell me," Rutledge said. "You vote, don't you?"

"I haven't done so yet," Jared replied. "I still have four years left on my current contract, so the bargaining agreement doesn't affect me the way it does some of the other guys."

Why were they beating around the bush? He doubted he'd been called in to discuss the potential lockout that had been mumbled about in the locker room. Jared couldn't stomach idle chitchat, not when his career was hanging in the balance.

He decided directness was the best approach. "Sir, Torrian Smallwood told me you know about my visiting Atlantic City."

Rutledge sat back in his chair, a pained expression flashing across his face.

Jared instantly regretted bringing up the subject. He could have used another minute or two to prepare himself for the blow he sensed was coming. He was about to lose his job.

"Jared, you know the team violated league policy when we decided to keep your gambling problem in-house. If management had followed protocol and reported that you'd made a bet on a game, you would be banned from ever playing in the NFL again."

"I know that," Jared said. "But I haven't made a single bet since then. I don't know who told you about my being at the casino—"

"It was an acquaintance. He was holding a Super Bowl party at the Rio and you were in the background of some of the pictures."

"I didn't gamble," Jared said. "I had a few drinks and I watched the game, but I never once laid down a bet. On anything."

"The agreement you signed with the team stated that you were not to visit any gaming establishments. You violated it just by being there."

Jared held his hands out, pleading, his heart banging against the walls of his chest. "I was in a really bad place mentally. It seemed as if things were spiraling out of control, and…I don't know…being at that casino was the only thing that felt familiar." Jared looked his boss in the eye. "I won't lie to you. I thought about it. I circled that craps table more than once, but in the end, I couldn't do it because I knew it was wrong. And since that day I have been kicking my butt trying to get in shape for next season."

"You had some rough days during the organized team activities."

"A few," Jared acknowledged. "Look, I know that I've done some things this off-season that would probably make getting rid of me seem like a practical option, but it would be a mistake. You're not going to find another player who will work harder."

Tom Rutledge settled back in his chair and rested his lips on his steepled fingers. The Super Bowl ring he'd won with the Dolphins glistened shiny and bright under the overhead lights.

"You know that Delonte Cannon has impressed the coaching staff," Rutledge said.

Jared forced himself to keep his voice even. "He's a good player."

"What would you do if we opened the season with him as a starter?"

Jared shifted in his chair and did his best to bank the fire that roared to life in his gut.

He cleared his throat and said, "I would go along with whatever the team thought was necessary to get to the championship game. If that means stepping back, then that's what I'll do. I can work with Delonte over the remainder of the off-season to make sure he's ready when the season opens."

Rutledge continued to peer at him. Slowly, one corner of his mouth drew up in a smile. "I requested this meeting alone with you for a reason, Jared. I wanted to see where your head was." He sat up in his chair and shuffled a couple of things on his desk. "I don't think you're ever going to gamble again."

"I won't," Jared agreed. "It's something I continue to fight, but I'm winning the battle, and I'll continue to."

Rutledge grabbed a stack of papers and tapped them into a neat pile. "Despite this slipup, I don't think it would be in the best interest of the team to dissolve your contract."

The anxiety that had settled into his shoulders released, and Jared was able to relax for the first time in twenty-four hours. "Thank you," he said. "I'm sorry for putting you in this position. Like I said, I was in a bad place at the time."

"I'm not blind to what goes on outside of this

organization, Jared. Everyone has their issues. It's my job to make sure those issues do not affect what happens on the field."

"They won't," Jared assured him. "If it means I'm not the starting cornerback, so be it. I'll learn to live with that."

"That decision is Coach Foster's."

"I understand." Jared nodded. He braced his hands on the armrest. "Are we done here?"

"We're done," Rutledge said. "Jared," he called, halting Jared as he rose. "You're a good player and one of the most selfless guys on the team. It's time you start understanding your worth. As much as I applaud you for willing to step back and do what you think is best for the team, you need to learn how to be a little more selfish. Don't just give your spot to Delonte Cannon. You earned your starting position. You make sure you keep it."

As he left the GM's office, the advice his boss had imparted volleyed back and forth in Jared's mind.

He needed to be selfish.

He'd been thinking along those same lines himself these past few weeks. He needed to take care of himself, and stop worrying so much about what others needed. The thought went down as smoothly as fingers down a chalkboard, but the more Jared ruminated on it, the more the words started to sink in.

Since the very first time he'd walk in on his crying mother and offered her the hem of his T-shirt to dry her eyes, he had made it his life's goal to take care of her. The same went for Samantha when she'd told him her sob story about growing up poor. And with Patrick when he'd needed money to get the Red Zone off the ground. His entire self-worth was based on what he did for other people.

What about what *he* needed? Who was there to take care of *him?*

A vision of solemn gray eyes blasted through Jared's mind.

Chyna's dogged determination to be self-reliant had inadvertently shown him that he didn't always have to be the one to give in order for a relationship to work. A relationship was about give and take, about two people giving of themselves and accepting what the other offered.

Jared's chest tightened with anticipation, urgency propelling him down the hallways of the Sabers training facility. He needed to get to Chyna. *Now.* He had to tell her he was ready to *let* her take care of *him,* but only if she would let him do the same.

Chyna tossed the tattered stuffed dumbbell several yards, laughing as Summer pounced on it and shook her head until more of the stuffing came out. Her puppy trotted back to the patch of grass where Chyna sat and pushed the dumbbell back into her hand. Chyna pitched it again. She knew how this game went, having played it too many times to count.

She leaned her head back and stared at the cloudless sky. She'd been waiting for panic to grip her, but ever since she'd exited the doors of Marlowe and Brown carrying her small box of belongings, she had felt nothing but peace.

Chyna recalled the look on Darla's face when she'd tendered her resignation. Instead of the disappointment— even anger—Chyna had anticipated from her supervisor, there had been admiration and just a small tinge of envy.

Her rational side continued to tell her that she'd made

a mistake by giving up the job she'd worked so hard to attain, but her heart refused to hear it. She'd done the right thing. Chyna forced herself to imagine life in two weeks, when she wouldn't get a paycheck. She clutched her stomach against the onslaught of fear.

It never came.

All she experienced was the excited rush of expectation that had washed over her the moment she had decided that life was too short to continue dipping her toe in the water. She was ready to dive in headfirst.

She thought back to the conversation she'd had with her father earlier this morning when she'd told her parents of her decision to quit her job. Sitting on the edge of her father's bed, Chyna had held his hand as tears dampened his cheeks. Barely able to look her in the eye, he had painfully owned up to the shame he'd harbored all these years for never having the courage to do more with his music. He'd admitted that he'd feared rejection and had been certain that if he had been discovered by a record label he wouldn't have been able to live up to people's expectations.

Then her father had confessed the most shocking truth of all, that he had been jealous of her. With tears clogging his words, her father acknowledged that he'd spent years discouraging her from pursing dance because he had been jealous of the way she had never let her dream die.

Chyna had been stunned. And angry. What kind of father could be jealous of his own daughter?

But as she'd stared at his tortured, guilt-laden face, a kinship she'd never felt with her father began to emerge. Remembering the envy she'd felt when Liani had first made the Saberrettes squad, Chyna understood how one could love a person yet still be jealous of their success. In that moment, she understood her father better than she ever had before, and with a kiss to his weathered cheek, she'd forgiven him.

Forgiving him had been easy, knowing that she was not going to end up like him.

Her father had allowed his fear of failure to paralyze his dream. Chyna refused to succumb to the same fate.

She'd wasted too many years living in fear. Fear that dancing would never provide enough money for her to support herself. Fear that if she allowed herself to pursue her dreams she would end up like her father, bitter, angry and wallowing in what could have been.

She'd lived in fear of…living.

Until Jared.

Jared had shown her what it meant to embrace life. He'd taught her to enjoy the moment. The freedom she'd felt this summer had been like nothing she'd ever experienced.

Chyna was done being afraid. She was ready to stop dreaming, and start *living*.

Whistling for Summer, she scooped the dog into her arms and gathered the chew toys sprinkled around her. Stuffing them into her backpack, along with Summer, Chyna took off for the subway and the only place where she wanted her new life to begin.

Jared rested his head against the mirrored wall of his building's elevator. After the grueling day he'd been through, he needed no less than an hour in the hot tub. The first day of practicing in full pads was always the hardest. It reminded him of why no one could play this game forever. The human body was not designed to withstand this kind of pain for an extended period of time.

The elevator dinged its arrival on his floor and the

doors opened. Jared walked out of the elevator and stopped short.

Chyna was sitting on the floor in his private foyer, her legs crossed, Summer in her lap. She looked up at him and hitched up her shoulders in a hapless shrug.

"I'm sorry," she said.

Relief washed over him like rain from heaven. Jared rushed to her, gathering her in his arms and pulling her to her feet. "How long have you been here?" he asked.

"A few hours," she said. "I needed to see you."

Still holding her hand, Jared opened the door to his condo and pulled her inside. The awkwardness that suffused the air created an uncomfortable ache in his chest. He hated that they were back here, at this stage where neither of them knew what to say.

"Can I get you something to drink?" he asked.

She shook her head. "I quit my job this morning," she announced.

Jared's head reared back in surprise, but before he could respond, she continued. "Landing that promotion has been my top priority for nearly six months, ever since the job was posted. I took on two extra classes this semester so I could finish my degree in time. I worked like a dog to show them that I was capable of handling all the work that would come with the new position. And for the past two weeks, I've cried myself to sleep at night because I'm so miserable."

Jared managed to stop himself from reaching for her. But just barely.

"I want to be happy," she said through the tears that had started to stream down her face. "And there are only two things that have made me happy—dancing and you."

"Chyna—"

She held her hands up, warding him off. "I have a proposition for you."

"Okay." Jared nodded slowly, unsure if he wanted to hear it.

"I'm willing to become your employee," she said.

"My what?"

"I will run the dance school and work as an instructor."

"Chyna, I bought the school for you."

"I know you did and it is the sweetest, most generous thing anyone has ever done for me. But it's too much." He tried to speak, but she cut him off. "I can't just allow you to *give* me the school. But I can buy it from you," she continued. "We can agree upon a price and you can keep a portion of my paycheck to go toward purchasing the school. And, no, you cannot sell it to me for a dollar," she finished.

Jared's mouth tipped up in a smile. She knew him well.

"Do we have a deal?" she asked.

"It doesn't seem as if there's room for negotiation," he said.

"That will come later, when we talk price. You should know that I plan to drive a hard bargain."

"I have no doubt about that," Jared said, reaching over and wrapping his arms around her. God, it felt good to hold her. "I'm looking forward to it."

She tilted her head up and pressed the sweetest, most delicious kiss to his lips. "So am I."

* * * * *

REQUEST YOUR FREE BOOKS!

2 FREE NOVELS PLUS 2 FREE GIFTS!

KIMANI™ ROMANCE

Love's ultimate destination!

YES! Please send me 2 FREE Kimani™ Romance novels and my 2 FREE gifts (gifts are worth about $10). After receiving them, if I don't wish to receive any more books, I can return the shipping statement marked "cancel." If I don't cancel, I will receive 4 brand-new novels every month and be billed just $4.94 per book in the U.S. or $5.49 per book in Canada. That's a saving of at least 21% off the cover price. It's quite a bargain! Shipping and handling is just 50¢ per book in the U.S. and 75¢ per book in Canada.* I understand that accepting the 2 free books and gifts places me under no obligation to buy anything. I can always return a shipment and cancel at any time. Even if I never buy another book, the two free books and gifts are mine to keep forever.

168/368 XDN FEJR

Name	(PLEASE PRINT)	

Address		Apt. #

City	State/Prov.	Zip/Postal Code

Signature (if under 18, a parent or guardian must sign)

Mail to the Reader Service:
IN U.S.A.: P.O. Box 1867, Buffalo, NY 14240-1867
IN CANADA: P.O. Box 609, Fort Erie, Ontario L2A 5X3

Not valid for current subscribers to Kimani Romance books.

Want to try two free books from another line?
Call 1-800-873-8635 or visit www.ReaderService.com.

* Terms and prices subject to change without notice. Prices do not include applicable taxes. Sales tax applicable in N.Y. Canadian residents will be charged applicable taxes. Offer not valid in Quebec. This offer is limited to one order per household. All orders subject to credit approval. Credit or debit balances in a customer's account(s) may be offset by any other outstanding balance owed by or to the customer. Please allow 4 to 6 weeks for delivery. Offer available while quantities last.

Your Privacy—The Reader Service is committed to protecting your privacy. Our Privacy Policy is available online at www.ReaderService.com or upon request from the Reader Service.

We make a portion of our mailing list available to reputable third parties that offer products we believe may interest you. If you prefer that we not exchange your name with third parties, or if you wish to clarify or modify your communication preferences, please visit us at www.ReaderService.com/consumerschoice or write to us at Reader Service Preference Service, P.O. Box 9062, Buffalo, NY 14269. Include your complete name and address.

KROM11B

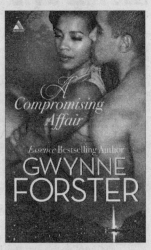

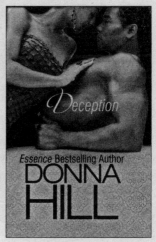